THE Last Love Song

T0349060

KALIE HOLFORD

BLACK STONE
PUBLISHING

Printed in the United States of America

First edition: 2024
ISBN 979-8-212-63801-2
Young Adult Fiction / Romance / LGBT

Version 2

Blackstone Publishing
31 Mistletoe Rd.
Ashland, OR 97520

www.BlackstonePublishing.com

*To Mum, Dad, and Ames for teaching me
the tune of listening to my own heart.*

To Alex for being there for every song.

*And to Leila who put this one on repeat
and made the words matter every time.*

PLAYLIST

Track 1: "Never Yours" by Tori Rose Peters

Track 2: "Wayward Lanes" by Fate's Travelers

Track 3: "Meet Me in the Lyrics" by Tori Rose

Track 4: "Chasing Sunsets" by Tori Rose

Track 5: "What If We" by Tori Rose

Track 6: "Head Forever to Your Dreams" by Tori Rose

Track 7: "H(our)glass" by Tori Rose

Track 8: "The One Time You Regret Me" by Tori Rose

Track 9: "Forever 18" by Mia Peters

"NEVER YOURS"

*Never-released song by late
country star Tori Rose Peters*

MIA

Grad gowns aren't made for climbing out windows. I learn this quickly as I sling one leg over my boyfriend's sill, tugging the hem of my robe, which has caught on the corner of the frame. It doesn't budge.

"Come *on.*" I pull a little harder and the fabric rips, the fraying threads just tangling worse. Since I have no intention of wearing it long, I tear a large piece from the robe, the new-found freedom a sweet escape.

Clearing the window and maneuvering across chipped roof tiles, I edge toward the rain gutter. All around me, salty air slips into the spaces between blinking stars, and the breeze closes in on Jess's seaside home. Just a little farther. Grab a branch of the leaning fir, avoid the needles, climb to the ground—clean and simple and goodbye-free.

Some days, I think I'd do anything for one less goodbye.

"Mia?" Jess's voice—both smooth and hesitant—comes from behind me. A glass of lemonade in each pale hand, he's out of his own cap and gown, ready for tonight in a V-neck and jeans. His dark hair is purposefully tousled, as artistically rendered as the rest of him.

"Oh, hey." My palms scrape against the bark.

He freezes one step into the room. "What are you doing?" Moving onto the first branch, I brace myself for a second escape. "I don't think this is working out."

"What?" He's at the window in two quick strides, and his hands fall to the same sill I left behind, fresh drinks sloshing over the cups' rims. Hurt coats his tone, and everything around us orbits the gravity he holds. "Just like that? You're leaving?"

Stray needles dig into my bare legs as I let the silence settle. After jumping the last couple feet to the ground, I press a hand to my chest, feeling the way my traitorous heart beats—the only part of me I can't control. I think my eyes apologize as I back away. Maybe some part of me hopes they do as a barely audible "sorry" sneaks past my lips.

For a second, everything falls from Jess's features—the anger, the hurt—and there's a steady resolve replacing it all in his gaze, like he expected this. As he should have.

Go. Now. Let him go. I wave to where he stands next to the da Vinci knockoffs that line his walls. My bike is only a foot away. *I can make it. I have to.*

"You're fooling yourself, Mia." His tone softens.

"Why? Because I'll never find someone like you?" I grip the handlebars a little too tightly and move the kickstand from the cement.

I've heard that before.

"No, because you're not willing to fall." Lips twisting, he pushes back—from the window and from me.

"I just jumped off a roof, Jess." If I don't acknowledge what he really means, I don't have to face that either.

He's not having it. "In love. You're not willing to fall in love." The poison abandons him, replaced with hope, and I freeze this time.

Those three words hung in his eyes when we gathered at the base of the stage just an hour ago with our screaming, cheering grad class. They were there when he hugged me, when he kissed me, when we pulled away from each other and he said *We're getting out of here*, like he didn't know I'm not. Like he didn't know I can't. Like he didn't know our little town of Sunset Cove is the only forever I've known and me staying here is as inevitable as the sun waking and setting each day. I tried to disappear before he could do this.

If I stay, he'll just end up leaving instead.

Sitting atop my bike and ringing the bell to the last beat I wrote for my best friend's band, I shake my head. My feet rise to the pedals. "I'm sorry." I don't look back again.

My cap soars off, caught in the Oregon coast's chilling wind. The phantom feeling of our principal placing my tassel from one side to the other—some sign I'm growing up and growing away—still plays before me. I'm better off without it, without another memory.

The uneven hem of my gown billows around me, and I pedal faster. A rainbow of beach cottages with verandas strung in glittering fairy lights blur in my periphery. The street is silent, the town is silent, the cars are gone—most to the beach where I'm heading later, where Jess is heading now, where we were supposed to go together.

I push that thought aside. There are more important things to do, answers I desperately need waiting for me at home. And he's as saved without me as I am without that cap and the missing piece of my gown. It doesn't matter if I'll miss his perpetually smiling lips or awful pickup lines. He's going to get out of here, go to art school, become the curator of some fancy museum. He's going to have an adventure, like the rest of our grad class.

He'll be fine.

And I'll be here.

Across from the little house my grandmothers built for us sixteen years ago, there's an inn we own and manage—Roses & Thorns. Beneath the neon red sign and the glowing rose that hangs over it—if I look close enough—I can still make out where it once said Peters, our last name.

Parking my bike outside the front door, I clasp the rose charm I've hung from the handlebars to remember Tori Rose: Sunset Cove's brightest star, and my mother.

One deep breath in, one quick breath out, and I force myself forward.

"I'm home," I say, sliding the door shut behind me, nerves settling at the vanilla candles Grams constantly burns. They fill the air down the hall that's lined with pictures of us through the years—but never ones of Mom.

"In the kitchen!" Nana calls from the other side of the wall.

Kicking off my boots and heading to the adjoined living room and kitchen, I trail my fingers over the peeling floral wallpaper. My footsteps slow and my shoulders unclench at the sight of two of the three people who hold together my entire world. They stand at the stove, stirring a pot of something that smells suspiciously like chocolate. Grams, laughing in the glow of the half-burnt-out lightbulb, holds the wooden spoon to Nana's lips for her to try. They're so in love, sometimes it hurts. That openness with each other hides all the things they won't share.

I know a few things for certain in our carefully constructed life together: they love me endlessly, they were broken by my mother's death, talking about her childhood hurts them, and they're all I've got.

"Hey, Mi Mi." Nana pulls me in fondly. The blue eyes she passed on to Mom and then to me are dancing.

"Sweetheart, try this." Grams takes another spoon from the pink, rose-shaped bowl, scuffed and treasured but with origins untold.

I do as she says, and its sweetness fills me with the sense of home they create.

"What is it?" I cover my mouth and swallow.

"Ganache." Grams takes the spoon Nana tasted from and tries it for herself. "Thought we'd make s'mores dip and sit out on the deck to celebrate. You've graduated, baby." It sounds like a congratulatory thing, but there's a sadness beneath it.

"Do you have time for that before the performance?" Nana asks, the last word broken.

"Yeah, of course." I shift from foot to foot, waiting for them to say something. I wait for them to tell me more—finally—about the elusive graduation gift my mother left me, the one I've anticipated in the void of every curbed question and answer this town didn't care to give.

All my life I've collected pieces of Tori Rose like breadcrumbs, lyrics like talismans, stories like safety nets. When I was eight years old, back from a school trip to her museum at the mouth of Sunset Cove, I sat at the dinner table between Grams and Nana, and I asked, "Who was Mom?"

They said what everyone said, practiced and hollow.

"A superstar."

"A wonder."

Never just a girl.

"No," I'd fidgeted. "Who was she really?"

And that was when, instead of detailing her, they told me she'd left me something. Something beyond college funds and a legacy I'd never amount to. Something concrete, something real, something I'd get the day I graduated.

A little piece of her that might answer everything I ached to know.

Here and now, Nana opens and closes her mouth, and I can count a million times like this that the story has almost slipped through. They constantly walk a tightrope between sharing her or protecting me. "Dessert will be ready soon." She lands on this. Conversation over.

The silence twists me up inside. They promised today. They've promised for years that I'd get this today. As much as her tragedy is the perpetual weight, the permanent elephant in each room we enter and exit, my grandmothers have not once in my life broken a promise to me.

"I'm going to get ready," I whisper, and they nod, turning back to the stove, exchanging a glance I can't translate into truths. Later. They'll tell me later.

Hopefully.

The aged hardwood creaks beneath my feet, and I slip into my room, casting one more look down the hall. There are no photos at this end of our home, only abandoned hooks, like they initially tried to decorate with her memories but couldn't keep them up. In those empty places, a collage of my own life plays before my eyes—hearts left half-opened, songs left unspoken, my love forever unsaid. All of those things were present even in Jess's wide brown eyes just a quarter of an hour ago.

Closing the hall off behind me, I fall back against my bedroom door. My closet is covered in concert posters my best friend, Britt, ripped out of magazines and lyrics Britt has scrawled and left for me to pen the melodies. My pink walls are at as much of a standstill as everything else here. A brown guitar hangs in the corner, something that Grams gave me when she couldn't bear to have it in her room anymore. I taught myself to play it with YouTube videos and insomnia. It's not Tori Rose's guitar—lost somewhere to the open road and her unfinished history—but it's a way to let out the music that haunts me. It sits right next to the hanging chair where I write chords after my grandmothers fall asleep.

My gaze falls upon my heart-patterned comforter, and my breath catches. There's a carefully wrapped package propped against my pillow, a curling ribbon tied around it.

With one more glance over my shoulder, I move so I'm standing in front of the rectangular gift. The wrapping paper is worn and creased, aged and faded with dust and years. Across its white background, little pink roses create a polka-dot design.

This is it. It has to be.

I peel back the top of the folded tag, and the loopy handwriting is identical to the penmanship on the notes that hang framed around town to memorialize the way Tori Rose left lyrics every time she stopped by a local pub or diner. It's something Britt and I do now, but we only leave notes for each other.

I clutch the gift tighter in trembling hands. My pulse races out of time with every one of her songs that echoes through my heart at the words. *Her* words. This is my mother's writing, and it's addressed to me:

Mia,

   Happy graduation, baby girl. Here's a little something for your Summer of Dreams from me to you. Do you dare?

                            Love,
                            Mom

MIA

Do you dare?

I slip my nails beneath the edges of the paper, exposing the corner of a pink book. The gold-embossed lettering catches the light of the star chandelier Grams designed and Nana built when I was six.

As I go to tear off the rest, a low laugh rises from down the hall, followed by a clatter, a reminder that my grandmothers are right out there with their pain and kindness and unshared stories. They've held my hands through scary movies, walked me to school rain or shine, hugged me goodnight and good morning, but they're just like me—they've never known how to say goodbye.

This isn't the place to open this. This isn't how to do this.

My purse sits on the hanging chair, and I grab it, sliding the still-partially-wrapped book in and leaving my room behind. Rushing down the hall, I pop my head into the kitchen.

"I forgot a book at the inn. I'll be back." I force out the lie, only pausing a second as Grams and Nana study me and each other, this time waiting to see if they'll talk about it, if they'll want to know what the gift was, if they'll offer to look with me. I wait to see if they're curious at all, and when they don't ask, I will my disappointment not to show.

"Okay, sweetie." Grams smiles softly. "Love you. S'mores dip may have to wait. Nana dropped the chocolate. See you after your party."

"I did *not*," Nana says.

My gaze falls to the splattered tiles. I can't help a small smile. "Is that okay? I won't be out too late."

"You'd better not be," Nana adds, but she's grinning too. "Have fun."

They don't say anything else even as Grams's eyes bore into my purse and Nana carefully avoids looking at it, stooping to wipe up the mess across the floor with her long salt-and-pepper hair falling out of its clip. The usual suffocating silence closes in at even the unspoken idea of this topic, but this time I have a way to find something out for myself.

Outside, the low-hanging clouds cover the moon at a whim, hanging in the still-light sky. I make my way across the half-filled parking lot. Tourist season in Sunset Cove doesn't start until mid-July, right around the time people will be shopping for college decorations, making final plans with high-school friends, and I'll be manning the desk of this place and sneaking chords between taking names for room reservations—chords only to be shared with Britt and her band, Lost Girls, who are performing tonight. Or to be shared this summer, anyway. There are only two months before Britt is determined to get out of here; she always has been, and now graduation isn't there to hold her back.

Nothing should hold her back.

I pull my purse tighter against my side.

The inn is quiet this week, and the guests are either settled in for the night or joining the party, because Sunset Cove celebrates few things quite as much as Tori Rose or graduation. The lobby sits empty as I cross it. My hand trails over the dusty fallboard of the grand piano I used to play to draw in visitors and for my grandmas every now and then before it got to be too painful, too real, too scary.

There are two halls from the main desk, one to the west and one to the east. I head west. It's way shorter than the other—barely its own wing—and doesn't wrap around to the pool in the middle or cherry blossoms in the back, but it holds more history. And it's closed to guests, to the public.

Before they literally moved their lives to our house at the front of the grounds, my grandmas lived in this wing with her. They gave me a key to it a long time ago, and it sits on a silver necklace with another that Britt and I found but still haven't discovered the door for. The key to this place is like a silent peace offering for all my grandmothers can't say, but that doesn't change what scratched floorboards and marker doodles on walls can't tell me.

Mom's bedroom sits to the immediate left: pale-pink curtains, unmade bed, vanity with lyrics scribbled across the mirror in Sharpie. There's a secret floorboard where she stashed an extra songbook with only one page filled, a pack of cigarettes, and a photo of her utterly in love with whoever's taking it, judging by her luminous smile.

But I don't go in there today. I don't go into my grandmas' old bedroom with all its pictures of her either—the ones that never made it into the house. I stop right outside the door that makes me ache the most: the nursery where I first slept, back when she was still here.

Glancing inside, I note the rose-gold walls and the lyrics along them that this town made a train station out of—*head forever to your dreams.* Sometimes I climb onto the rocking chair in the corner when I can't sleep, teetering softly, and I pretend it's her rocking me.

"Hey, Mom," I whisper, tracing a framed tour poster on the wall across from the room. My reflection catches in the glass, and there's the same pale skin, blue eyes, wild blond hair. Enough for this town to know who I am, but with nothing truly shared between us. It's like a game of Spot the Difference. The smug lilt of her lips and the slight downturn of mine. The spark in her eyes and the hurt in my own. The freckles on my shoulders and the hint of a tattoo carrying off her collarbone. Bravery in her gaze and cowardice in mine.

This time, I make sure to be careful with the paper despite the part of me that wants to rip it open. I peel it back slowly, keeping it intact, and I let the sheet fall to the dark hardwood floor as the book is fully revealed. *Journal* is printed in bold across the cracking pink-leather cover, tied together by a ribbon with roses on it. The pages are slightly yellowed and only the first ten are there.

Flipping through, I note the seven envelopes tucked inside. Their hues form a rainbow, and they're stacked where the rest of the paper should be but was ripped out. Each envelope says *Open Here* and verses from her songs are scrawled across them, moving through the albums of her career. Above that, there's my name.

I return to the front of the book where looping handwriting graces the spaces between the lines, the same as on the gift tag. My hands are as unsteady as my pulse when I go to read.

Mia,
> *There's so much I want to say to you. And I thought to myself of how to tell you these things. How to be here, in your life, without really being here. So I compiled this*

*for you. Call it a hunt, if you will. It'll take you around
Sunset Cove, to the spots where I found the most hidden
magic.*

*Each envelope has a hint on the outside in the lyrics
from one of my songs. When you think you've found the
place to match, open it. Do this seven times and find the
pattern. The clue inside each one will lead you to the
missing pages of my diary.*

*I'm sure there's an urge to open it all now. But I
promise it'll make so much more sense if you do it one by
one before putting it together.*

*I hope we'll know each other by the end of this. I hope
that soon you'll know me, and I can tell you my story one day.*

Love,

Mom

My next inhale is sharp, and I'm unable to let go of the leather
cover and those ripped pages and the seven multicolored envelopes
that make a rainbow of everything I've ever needed. It's a hunt, a
journey, an entire diary's worth of stories to find out about her life.

She *wants* me to know her. My mother did this for me. She
left me something the rest of this town can't own or hide. She's
here, in these pages.

This really is my way of finding out everything: who she was,
who my father was, why she fell from stardom, and whatever
message she had. This is the advice I've longed to hear from her.
I can recognize her voice from a thousand interviews I watch
late at night, but I have never heard it as clearly as in this note
on the first page—the one addressed to me.

I turn to the next page in the handful of those that remain
before the rest are gone and the envelopes take their place.
There's what looks like a sample, a first entry, but my phone

buzzes in the pocket of the lavender dress Britt and I picked out earlier this week. Britt's name appears on my screen, along with the contact photo I took the year we rode the tilt-a-whirl at the summer festival after having two bags of cotton candy.

> You coming??
>
> Mi
>
> Mi
>
> Miaaaaaaaa
>
> Are you still breaking up with him?
>
> Did they give it to you? Did you get the gift?

I tap out a quick text, and after holding on a second longer, put the diary back in my purse. Promises aren't something I'm willing to break either. Not when they're to Britt; never when they're to Britt.

> I'm on my way.

The shouting reaches me before the glow of the bonfire and before the swaying blur of dresses and ripped jeans. Leaving my bike in an empty parking spot, I toss what remains of my grad gown into the trash at the edge of the lot and tuck my key necklace back into my dress. Spotlights beckon across the shore, shifting from pink to gold. Somewhere backstage, Britt's waiting for me, and my pace quickens. I'm flying to reach her.

As I weave through my classmates, a guy I recognize from Lit gestures wildly with a red cup, and I dodge the splash zone. Relieved, I run up the steps to where Britt stands, laughing and chatting with the other Lost Girls: drummer Amy Li and pianist Sophie Jordain. The three of them have been playing together since the ninth-grade talent show, and I've been writing the tracks to accompany Britt's lyrics for about that long, coming to watch every show and practice but never getting up onstage.

It's better for everyone that way.

Britt's eyes flit over my expression, and her brows arch slowly as she peels away from the group. Amy and Sophie wave, swaying into one another in giggles.

Then Britt's nudging my arm, smiling my way, making my head this mix of light and racing and dizzy that she always seems to manage. Her dark curls are pinned up with Saturn-shaped bobby pins, and her light-brown skin is freckled with gold sparkles that match the stitches on her dress.

"How was the breakup? Did it make the top three?" she asks first, but I can see in the slight pursing of her lips that it isn't the real question on her mind. The diary seems to burn through my bag, begging me to share with her what my mother did for me.

"Very funny. Way to make me sound superficial." I lean up against the large speaker next to her, smoothing the lacy folds of my skirt. I don't know what I'm trying to prove to myself, what Aza, Mason, Jenna, and Jess couldn't tell me. All this time chasing something and not one of them made me feel the way that—

Maybe love isn't something I'm meant for just like music isn't. Britt's the only person, besides my grandmas, I ever thought I could say *those* words to—the ones Jess tried to tell me and I ran from—but it's not a feeling the two of us are meant to have together. We learned that the hard way.

"You know that's not what I meant." She nudges my arm again, a silent check-in, and it's all I can take.

I lean my head softly on her shoulder, careful not to put too much of my weight on her, and Britt squeezes my hand. Her clothes are scented with lavender and the ocean breeze, and I once threw out a whole song because the scents wove their way into the verse. Now, I stick to chords, not lyrics.

"You excited?" I whisper into her shoulder.

"For this? Always," she says, her voice shifting, a far-off quality seeping into it the closer she gets to stepping out beneath the lights. She shifts so her head rests on mine. "Why don't you join us? It's the last high-school show. Come on, Mia." There's something else in her tone now, too, something urgent.

But the last time she and I were on a stage together, the spotlights weren't the only flashing lights we saw. *She's better off without me.*

"Next time," I say because that's what I always say—not a promise since we both know it can't happen.

She stiffens as the pep band finishes their set and our vice principal heads onstage to introduce Lost Girls, telling a bad knock-knock joke to the crowd. "That's what I need to talk to you about."

"What?" I tilt my chin up, meet her eyes, and her breath fans my lips in the way it always does before something happens. We always let something happen.

Her frown brings back everything we can't have, all the reasons I run to hearts like Jess's only to disappear and break them. Britt and me? We're the kind of could-have-been love story even I don't understand.

We've slipped up a few too many times—seven to be

exact—looking at each other just like this, pushing forward past this. Every beginning of us is foggier than the last, but between each other's breakups, we fall into something of our own. It never lasts long, and it never gets serious. It fades when life gets in the way, then we dance around it. We've always known she was leaving and I was staying, that she needed something outside this town and I could only be here—that the music called her and trapped me.

Us being more than whatever we are was never possible. After all, how would we ever work if her eyes are set on the road and my feet are planted here, gaze still sifting through the past?

The last thing I need is to let myself get entirely wrapped up in someone else who's sure to leave me behind.

The vice principal's voice breaks through memories, rising as she says, " . . . introducing Lost Girls!"

When I turn back to Britt, shaking myself free of everything we were, her gaze is wide, mouth set in that determined way it does when she's steeling her resolve. "We'll talk after the show?"

"Yeah, of course," I say, and I watch her shoulder her sky-blue guitar and go to huddle with Amy and Sophie.

They've played football games and dances and birthday parties, and at the end of this summer, they're going to play for the world—not just our little corner of it.

The beat starts, one I know like every freckle on the back of Britt's hand. It's one of the first ones we wrote together for Lost Girls.

"Loveless Stars."

Over the years, every time I've played this song to myself, I've just broken up with someone or been about to. Now, Britt's voice, low and powerful, spreads over the beach, and the tears burn, but I refuse to let them fall.

This evening, sitting in the wings and watching her assured

walk from one side of the stage to the next, I know the only way I'm going to get a piece of that, a piece of who *I* was born to be, is to turn the pages my mother penned. Pulling out the diary and flipping to where I left off, I settle against the make-shift stage and I start on the trail Tori Rose left for me.

TORI

1989

It all began the summer I told everyone to call me Tori Rose.
When I had a secondhand guitar and a purse full of dreams.

It began when I knew two things absolutely:

I was stuck in Sunset Cove.

I wanted out.

David's hands adjusted nervously around the waist of my
floral dress as my moms took their thousandth photo. The cor-
sage on my wrist itched, and I leaned back into him with a sigh,
humming Dolly Parton.

Arms relaxing, he laughed. "What song's that?"

"If you don't know, maybe you shouldn't be taking me to
prom."

I smirked over my shoulder. His green eyes lit up like spotlights. With tousled blond hair, a July tan, and his tie askew,
he was still my beach-bro best friend. Just dressed up in a suit.
A ridiculous silver suit. With a *bow tie*.

"One more," Mama said (for the fifth time) as Mom waved
the latest Polaroid, fanning herself in the evening sun. The

broken pink sign over our inn winked, as always, across the too-empty parking lot with the *r* in *Peters* burned out.

"Tori, look here." Mama laughed.

"We're going to be late." Usually a late entrance wouldn't faze me, but the music was waiting.

"Hon, let them go," Mom said.

Mama blinked, lowering the camera, smoothing a hand over her curls. "You're so grown up." Her dark skin and soft eyes made her look like one of the princesses from the fairytales she wrote.

Mom waved me over, the sea breeze sending her auburn braid across her pale cheeks. Somewhere in the distance, the waves left the shore as they hugged me goodbye.

"Be smart," Mom said.

"Sing a song for me," Mama said.

I nodded to both. I only agreed to one (but they didn't need to know that).

"You too," Mom said to David. "Have fun."

"Yes, ma'ams." He grinned and extended his elbow, all gentlemanly, to me. I shoved it away, giggling, and we took off.

My guitar bounced against my back with each stride. The inn fell behind us. It was the place my family had come back to this town to buy and run. I raced away from it like I'd wanted to since we arrived.

David jogged backward along the sidewalk, letting out a loud whoop and pumping his fist in the air. "Almost done! Prom, here we come!"

I sped to catch up, stumbling once when we passed the sign leading out of town. On it, the ocean was depicted in peeling paint.

Arced above the artwork: Welcome to Sunset Cove, where dreams rise. Your journey starts here.

I'd never seen a clearer lie. But little could happen in a place where only the tide changed and dreams set with the sun.

"Tori?" David skidded to a stop. "You coming?"

The sign sparked a fire in me. With graduation only a week away and prom tonight, I needed to find something more—how to rise for real.

"Yeah," I said quickly, and I took his moment of concern to gain the lead.

Prom was at the Horizon. Our grad class was only fifty students, but they already spilled out the doors onto the street, which was filled with shops and wildflowers. This was the only good diner in town, and it was strung with winking fairy lights. The kara-oke machine I ruled every Friday was front and center, but the stage was otherwise empty. The crowd was full.

Knee-length and floor-length dresses. Brightly colored suits. Dancing and singing to the boombox that barely made a sound over the crowd.

At least there was music.

I twirled into the masses. Winked David's way and lured him onto the dance floor. It took less than a second for him to join.

We'd been best friends since we were five, until my family left to care for my grandma. A time marked by a couple lost letters and a stream of love songs at my fingertips. We fell right back together when I returned two months ago. The mischief in his eyes was the only interesting thing here. I put my hands on his hips, jiving to the music.

"Think that girl's checking you out," I teased, nodding my chin toward the back where a brunette was studying his (en-thusiastic but awful) moves.

His fingers laced through mine, and he spun me. "Already

got a date." This time he winked. I wasn't, really. We'd both agreed on that (though mostly me). There'd been this one time, right when I got back, that we'd kissed. A little tipsy. But I'd ended it. It wasn't right. He was the past and he was this town. I told him I was ready to dance to the next song.

He needed to skip to a new track too.

"I'm going to see Linnea. Go talk." I nudged him.

Rolling his eyes, he squeezed my fingers. I squeezed back and walked over to the counter where the owner's daughter, Linnea, stood. She was a few years older than me. Pinning up her black hair, she waved before I even made it over.

"Tori Rose?" she said, and I loved her for it. She was one of the people here who saw me as what I was going to be.

Not Tori Peters. Tori Rose. The singer. The dreamer.

The *star*.

Rose was technically my middle name, but it ran deeper than that. In a town too gray to let the colors of the rainbow shine, my moms had their first date. Mom showed up at Mama's door with a dozen pink roses, and Mama's fairytale-loving heart knew she was the one. They'd run away together. In my family, roses were the start of an unapologetic love story. One that took the lead and pulled their hearts in its direction. One stronger than I'd ever seen. I wanted a love like that. To last. To guide me and hold me close. Music was the suitor I'd chosen.

Tori Rose seemed like a good start.

I leaned against the counter and asked Linnea, "Where's the music?"

She gestured to the boombox David was bopping near, having already moved on from that girl. "Right there."

"The live music?"

"Guy canceled last minute. I got someone else, but I dunno if he'll show. Didn't recognize him."

Not recognizing someone in Sunset Cove was rarer than winning the lottery. "Oh yeah?"

Her eyes fell to my guitar. "You're the only person I know who would lug that thing to prom. Tell you what, if he bails too, the stage is yours tonight."

My heart soared. She returned to wiping the counter until I made my way back to David. Even without the band, I found my rhythm in every song. Linnea's gaze kept darting to me, and I swore any second she was going to say go ahead.

The stage was mine. Even if it was in Sunset Cove, it was something.

Then the mic shrieked. Everyone looked to where a tall boy with brown ringlets tied into a low ponytail stood. He was fixing the mic stand (which was a head too low for him) and wincing at the feedback it expelled.

I studied his angular features. Blue eyes. Tanned skin. He was about our age. The hint of a tattoo was on the back of his neck that earned him a couple weird looks and my immediate admiration. Even though he'd shown up just in time to ruin my song, I wanted to get closer to see what was inked across him.

"Who's that?" I whispered.

"Your next crush?" David said.

"Oh, screw you."

He chuckled, and I nudged him again.

Getting the mic to the right height, the singer spoke, "Hey y'all. Sorry for the delay." He had a smooth Southern accent, and I exchanged a glance with David. Who *was* this? "Came with Cash here." He patted the red acoustic on his back, a matching guitar pick between his fingers. *Oh.* He'd named his guitar after Johnny Cash. "I'm Patrick Rose. Thought I'd play you a song."

Cheers echoed, but I didn't move. "Did he just say Rose?"

Patrick *Rose*.

"Think it's fate?" David asked.

Before I could answer, Patrick smiled at the karaoke machine and stepped in front of it. He played the opening chords of "Don't Stop Believin'." And he *sang*. His voice was a state of in-betweens, between high and low, gravelly and smooth. Even Linnea stopped what she was doing. It's not like we hadn't heard "Don't Stop Believin'" a million times over—I swore Sunset Cove's radio knew three songs, all of them by Journey—but it was just the way Patrick told the story. Like it was *his*.

As he finished the first chorus, I stepped forward. This song could be mine too.

The dancing had started when stilted silence disappeared. I didn't hear anything but the music and crossed the room. I knew what I needed to do as if some cosmic force propelled me.

"What are you doing?" David asked. But he knew the answer as I reached the steps leading up the stage and took the other mic.

Patrick's mouth went slack.

I swung my guitar to my front, fingers moving to frets.

He sobered quickly, rolling with it. Until I sang. I had a great voice. I knew it. Quickly and all too obviously, he knew it too. Someone wolf-whistled. Someone else rolled their eyes, like people did when I was too loud in class or at parties. Oh well.

The song became separate from the prom. I pulled the mic closer, stepped to the edge of the stage, tossed my hair, and walked the line before turning back to Patrick. His eyes were only on mine. He was visibly shaken, unsteady in his sneakers on the rickety stage. Whether that was because we sounded so *good* or that I joined his song, I didn't know.

I didn't care.

The last of the chords faded without us breaking gaze, and applause came next. He crossed the stage to me.

Tori Rose took over every piece of Tori Peters as I extended a hand. He took it, shaking it, still looking me up and down.

"Patrick," he said. "My name's . . . Patrick Rose."

"Nice to meet you, Patrick."

"And . . ." He cleared his throat. "You are?"

"Tori," I said, and the boombox interrupted our moment. Still, he watched. Now *he* was waiting. It thrilled me. But mystery left them all hooked, so I hopped down from the stage.

"Tori what?" he said after me.

I tossed a glance back over my shoulder. "Rose."

By the time I got home I was half-drunk (Linnea left the counter unattended, and David and I served her secret stash of wine to the crowd). Meanwhile, the inn slept, its few patrons already in bed.

The room was dark. A lamp dwindled at the heart of the lobby. Mom would be asleep and Mama would be reading, bedroom door cracked open so I could crawl between them and tell them everything when I walked into the suite we'd claimed.

But I didn't make it that far. I settled onto the bench of the ancient piano, and I propped my guitar beside me.

I recalled it all. The way his lips spoke fairytales and his eyes spoke much less chivalrous things. Sparks of moments. His smile. His voice. The hints of that tattoo, which I'd caught a peek at. It was as telling as his name. An intricate black rose.

Miracles didn't happen in Sunset Cove. Fate didn't rear its head here. But it had. This was a sign. I'd make it a sign.

Sliding the fallboard up, I stroked the piano's keys. "Don't Stop Believin'" came out, and the music wrapped around me. It always tempted me with something illicit. Every time I came running back to it. A story. A promise. A dream.

Closing my eyes, I whisper-sang. I couldn't wake this town, but I felt woken up within it. Streetlights and midnight trains.

Anywhere. Exactly where I needed to be.

And, as if the universe was on my side, a voice joined me. I blinked and there he was. Patrick Rose. In a crisp T-shirt, acid-washed jeans, hair out of the ponytail, but his stranger's face unmistakable.

His voice was gentler than I'd kept mine. He made his way across the lobby, and I held his gaze again. Our melodies wound together. I didn't make a move until the song was over. The second it was, I stood to rest my arms atop the piano.

"You following me or something?" I stared through lowered lashes.

Two times.

One night.

Fate.

He nodded down the hall. "Crashing here, actually. I checked in right before prom. I didn't know you were staying too."

"We run the place."

"Oh."

"So you just thought you'd interrupt my song?" My painted nails tapped along C major.

He grinned, smile as charming as the rest of him. "Seemed only fair. You did interrupt mine first."

"Oh yeah?" My heart beat a second too fast. "Well, song's over. Goodnight then." I let my shoulder brush his as I passed. Daring him to make the first move. His fingers gently touched mine.

"Tori, wait."

TRACK 2
"WAYWARD LANES"

Acoustic track feat. Sara Ellis and Tori Rose
from Once Upon an I Told You So, *1990*
album by Fate's Travelers

MIA

I flip to the next part of the story, but there's only those seven envelopes and the lyrics that grace them.

"No no *no*." I turn the paper over like there will be words within the lines, hidden in the margins, but there's nothing left but her hunt.

This story, her history, shows her just as I envisioned, just as everyone alluded: bold and true and determined—everything I'm not. She knew what she wanted. She knew where she was going and why. The surety of her words, the things she tells me here—behind the cameras when no one's watching—fill the spot in my rib cage where the guilt usually makes its home.

While I have this, in some way, I have her here with me.

This is how she started. This is her real story, from *her*. I knew Patrick existed; I knew that their careers, and possibly love lives, were speculated by the media to have been intertwined. But no one knows how they ended . . . and I'd never seen David Summers mentioned in the press at all. Is one of them my dad? What is she trying to say? Why spread it out?

I take the first envelope from the stack as Amy launches into a drum solo onstage, Lost Girls' music wrapping around me like a warm blanket, like it always does. The envelope is scarlet, and my mom's loopy cursive forms my name just above the lyrics and the *Open Here*, more intricately written than any of the other words, with a heart dotting the *i*.

The lyrics of its clue are from the first and only album—named after their hit single—by her once-band, Fate's Travelers, full of longing and bittersweet, unapologetic remorse in all its juxtaposition.

> *In a trail of careless maybes, I find myself undone,*
> *Photos tinted at corners, nostalgia bleached by the sun,*
> *Still staring at the places we marked our names,*
> *Here and all around towns.*
> *And they always did say I'm the one you couldn't bring home,*
> *Ship cast out to sea, grave of regrets all my own,*
> *But every ending I go through, I begin once again,*
> *With the taste of each sea, and your hand in my hand.*

The song is "Wayward Lanes" and has subtle references to different small-town locations including an actual structure at the very edge of Sunset Cove. Beyond all the artificial recollections of Tori Rose—on a jagged outcropping of rock, near the practically retired theater that turns out one show about every five years—there's a house.

Britt and I found it last year.

I was in math class, halfway through a quadratic equation, when Britt called my name from the door. She told my teacher they wanted me at the office, and we raced outside to her car and took off. She drove so far, so fast in our anticipation—we became one with the salty breeze.

She pulled up at the edge of Sunset Cove, where there's nothing much but rocks and sky and sea—and that house. It was small and leaning, abandoned, with a street sign hidden by twisting vines. We found a key under the mat, but it didn't work. It's now the second key I wear around my neck alongside the one for the western wing of the inn. Every once in a while, I'll pass an odd door and I'll try it just to see if it fits.

Cheers echo from the crowd beyond the stage, pulling me away from my thoughts, and Lost Girls takes a bow. Britt leads the way offstage beneath the spotlight that always lingers, flushed and grinning, and Amy and Sophie hurry down the side steps to join the party.

"Hey." I shut the book, shoving it back into my purse, turning over the image of that house as I meet Britt's eyes.

"What was that?" She leans next to me against the speaker, nodding toward my bag, never missing a thing.

"What did you want to tell me?" I ask right back.

Gazes locked, we stare each other down. She tilts her head to the side, a small challenge, and I almost smile at the gesture, folding my hands in my lap. My cheeks heat under her stare, but I refuse to break. As the ocean air stings my eyes, she blinks first and sighs.

Our mutual stubbornness got to the point where staring contests have become our only decision-making method. She usually beats me—something's off.

"Fine," she says, taking a deep breath, and my chest tightens as she plays with the silver charm bracelet her cousin mailed her from Colombia for her eighteenth birthday. There are three charms on it: a guitar from her parents, a heart from her cousin, and a star from me.

"Britt? What's wrong?" I stop myself from scooting closer.

"We got a gig," she says, tucking a stray curl behind her ear.

The chords of the set she just finished pound against my rib cage, and there's a hesitant excitement beneath her nerves that she sends away in an exhale until her assuredness is all that's left.

"That's great." I swat her arm. "When? Where? Can I come watch?"

"It's in Nashville. We're leaving in a week. And yeah, I want you to come." She angles toward me, and now that the words are out, her eyes hold elusive possibilities, brighter than the sequins dotting her skirt and the lights she just left.

Another shout rises from the crowd in my silence, and she doesn't look away, but I do.

"Mia," Britt says, and she's so close. Her voice is a whisper, but I can hear it as well as every scream from our grad class. "Come with us. We've always written the songs together. You know the set by heart. Your . . . your voice is . . ." She trails off and it's so uncharacteristic, her not pushing on to get to her point like the student body president she spent our entire high-school experience as. That's what tells me how badly she wants me to say yes.

A *week*.

For just this tiny millisecond, I close my eyes tight to hold in the tears and imagine it. The first time I ever sang for someone was with Britt, beneath her willow tree. She looked right at me and said, "your voice is like the sunrise." She's always been the poet of the two of us.

"A week?" is what comes out, aloud this time. The speaker vibrates against the backs of our legs, and we shift over so we're sandwiched by curtains and abandoned grad gowns just like the one I threw out. "Britt that's . . . that's . . . amazing."

And it is. This is everything she's ever wanted. In a town built on music, she made her own and has always planned to go to Nashville.

"Are you . . ." I hesitate. "Are you coming back after?" *Or is this it?* I want to ask too.

She drops her gaze, and it's my answer. She's not just going to Nashville. She's leaving Sunset Cove.

We were supposed to have summer. Two months of helping her pack, searching all the thrift stores in town to bargain hunt for her cross-country journey, soaking it all in and prolonging this. I thought maybe by then I'd learn how to say goodbye to her, of all people, that maybe it'd be easier with those memories. I push away how eerily her journey follows the tune of my mother's.

She continues, "We're running out of next times. You can't keep just putting it off. It's now. We're doing this now, and we'd love for you to come and really join, but we can't wait."

"I—"

"Mia, I know you love it. I know you want it."

"I can't." I shake my head slowly at first and then faster and take a step back. The music tangles up inside of me, twisted with each vein and artery and my stupid, careless heart.

Her eyes shout *Keep telling yourself that*, but she only says, "Think about it. Really think about it without the fear and the lies and the telling yourself you can't have it."

"No." I keep shaking my head. "No. Britt, I can't do what she did. My grandmas and the inn and the story and her end and she's this town and last time we performed and I don't know but I don't want to wreck and . . ." I press a fist to my lips. I will not cry I will not cry I will *not* cry. "I don't want to wreck it."

I can't be trusted with a piece of her dreams.

Her arms are around me before the last word is out of my mouth, and she pulls me close. "Mi." It's all she says, but I wrap my arms around her too, and everything feels a little more right with the universe.

"I'm sorry," I tell her, and she doesn't say *It's okay*, because it's not. She doesn't say *Forget it*, because neither of us will. She doesn't say any of the empty words people say in response to apologies, and I don't want them. I add, "You're going to do amazing. So, a week. A week before you're on your way to becoming a star." A week left of her, here, in Sunset Cove. A week left before she leaves.

A week.

The diary in my purse feels heavier somehow.

She laughs. "You'd better believe it." She turns to leave, motioning for me to join her. "Think about it," she says.

And I blame it on her freckles and smile and the music she just sang, but I whisper, "Okay," even though I can't, and it's the first time I've ever really lied to her.

Now more than ever, I need my mother to help me find the truth.

"So what was it?" Britt rests on her back, curls splayed around her and knees raised to the starry sky. "When are you going to tell me what your mom gave you?"

I sit crisscross in front of her, looking out at Sunset Cove from the inn's roof. The peaks of cottages are illuminated by streetlights, and the red glow of our sign, blinking in the dark, sends a sheen across our spot on the roof and everything below.

Once Grams and Nana figured out the chocolate debacle, they invited Britt's family to share it. My grandmothers are close with her parents, and we've been stuck together since we were infants, the music between us being what shifted our relationship from proximity to choice. The music that's fading out in just a week, when she leaves and I stay behind.

In her first entry, my mom called her Sunset Cove best friend—David—the past. Is that all I'll be when I'm no longer in Britt's present, much less her future?

Downstairs in the lobby, sitting near the piano but never on the bench, Nana and Grams chat with Mrs. and Mx. Garcia as guests returning from the party ask for fresh towels and everyone calls it a night. Britt and I slipped up here half an hour ago, but the scents of the campfire still slip across the parking lot from our house.

The part of me that wants to share it with her wars with the part of me that wants to convince her I'll be fine.

"It's a diary." I shift so I'm facing her. "It's *her* diary."

She sits up now. "Did you read it?"

"It's not all there. It's . . . it's a hunt." I pull it out, having not parted with my purse since I found the book, and I hand it to her.

A silent agreement passes between us as she takes it in her hands, thumbing through the pages, mouth gaping a little more with each sentence she skims. My pulse leaps, seeing that wonder on her features, that endless curiosity, seeing that the real story, my mom's story, is something that she thinks matters more than the legends and attractions Tori Rose has become too.

When she's finished, the resounding snap of the book closing fills the night.

She gives it back to me. "Why didn't you say something sooner? This is huge."

You told me you're leaving before I could. "I didn't know what to say. I don't know what this *means,* but it's her. It's her. I read those first pages, and that first song, it references the house we found."

"I know." Britt studies my expression so intently.

"She's got something to tell me."

"Maybe she's trying to tell you to chase the music," Britt breathes, and I shake my head.

"I . . . she . . . You know where it left her." I press my fingers to my temples, lying back again when she does.

No one really knows how Tori Rose died. Not the news, not the people here. It's another mystery—along with her life story, her chosen partner, and the final whereabouts of her treasured guitar. All the things that make a *life*, not just a celebrity. I always assumed it was a car crash when my grandmas said—in one of those times growing up they'd accidentally reveal something about her—that she never made it back from her *Regret You* tour. I always assumed she went too far. After all, even in this small piece of her truth, she called the music illicit. But the theory of a large accident seemed unlikely. It wasn't something that would've remained so well hidden. Not with how bright she shone, not with how mysteriously she fell.

All I know is that the music is what took her back to the open road, the music is what caused her to keep running, keep flying, and die away from her own family. The music took her from us. The music kept my mom, not me.

"I do know," Britt says. "But here's your answer. Here you go. It's what you've been waiting for. So stop thinking about it. Let's do it. Let's solve it."

"You want to help?" I shift toward her too fast and almost crash into her. She steadies me with a hand on my arm, and we're only a breath apart.

I'm not sure who moves back first.

We've listened to every Tori Rose track together, used to sing the songs into random household items, back when the music didn't scare me. If Britt wants to do this together, we can finish it before she leaves. I can figure out where to go from here, and through my mother's message, how to tell her everything I need to say.

"I'm here as much as I can be," Britt adds. "As long as I can be."

I let that sink in. Britt is offering to discover my mother with me, and I *want* to share this with her. I want her to be here for this.

"Play the song," Britt says, knowing my answer to *this* offer already. "Maybe it'll spark something."

I open Spotify and place the phone on my stomach, and we listen, both of us on our backs, studying the sky, not feeling so alone knowing we're going to do this together. The intro music is soft, careful, wrapped around the slight creaking of a swing. The piano crescendos right before it stops, everything stops, and her voice comes through, open and raw.

> *They say count your blessings. I don't listen.*
> *Listen close, but I never learn.*
> *They say remember those words, so I forget them.*
> *He says come see this, and I went to him.*
> *Our footsteps found each other's paths.*
> *Before the ocean even knew our names,*
> *I lingered when you looked my way.*
> *Didn't know this was our last day.*
> *I sit on the swing and brush over our lines,*
> *Try to remember when you were all mine.*
> *In a trail of careless maybes, I find myself undone,*
> *Photos tinted at corners, nostalgia bleached by sun,*
> *Still staring at the places we marked our names,*
> *Here and all around towns.*
> *And they always did say I'm the one you couldn't*
>   *bring home,*
> *Ship cast out to sea, grave of regrets all my own,*
> *But every ending I go through, I begin once again,*
> *With the taste of each sea, and your hand in my hand.*

I restart the song, replay it until it reaches that part again. The second verse goes into the swing and tale behind it, but that's not the focus of what she penned as my first clue.

"Do you think it actually is that house?" I take another turn looking at this envelope and rub my thumb along the key that rests over my collarbone. Maybe we missed something.

Britt shakes her head. "I don't think so. We looked around that whole place when we went. There's something else. It's at the beach, though. Somewhere there."

"There's got to be more here." I close Spotify and open YouTube, pausing only to note the video Britt posted—time-stamped last night—on her channel. She's been constructing a platform with original music since she was thirteen, a way to get a foot in the door of an industry where white-bro country takes up more than its fair share of airtime; where female singers aren't played back-to-back; where tracks about girls kissing can be removed from rotation. There, she sings songs with English and Spanish tied together about girls who love girls and people who challenge the standards set before them.

"What is it?" She leans over my shoulder, and I scroll past it.

"Just looking at something," I whisper, saving it to watch later.

I enter the song's name in the search bar and select the music video for "Wayward Lanes."

Under a sepia filter, it begins on the beach, just like we remember. The band—all five members—walks along the shore, heads down the coastline, their summer attire wrinkling in the breeze. Footprints trail behind them and five other sets—without people to make them—walk beside them. The tide comes to cover the prints with each step, erasing the path they take as they move on and apart.

The whole first verse flickers between small towns, friends laughing, a couple dancing on a deck overlooking the sea. I know one of these five places is Sunset Cove, and I catch glimpses of it fading in and out. A Fate's Travelers wiki likes to claim this song is about the band being homesick, but it's the one track the band themselves never even hinted at the meaning behind.

As the chorus starts, the focus returns to the couple again, and there's a light behind them, gleaming. It's a lighthouse, and it has to be Sunset Cove's, with its old fishing nets hung on the walls, fading pink paint, crates against the right side to hide a hole in the wall that someone made on Cove High School's senior beach day in the eighties and which was never repaired. No one knows exactly how it happened.

The light is on like it hasn't been in years. Once a port, Sunset Cove no longer needs the sea to be its guide, not when it holds on so tightly to its star.

But as the video reaches the end of the verse my mom wrote on the envelope, it zooms out all the way, looking at a skyline. I pause it, staring out at where the beach sits and the lighthouse looms over the far-off ocean in real time, when something catches my eye.

I glance at Britt, and her gaze widens as her fingertips graze my elbow. I keep my eyes on the view, away from where her hand rests—because we're best friends and touched like this before we ever touched like *that*. Together, we guide my phone up at the same time. All thoughts disappear as the skyline from the screen matches perfectly with the view of town from the inn's roof.

In the video, those two figures dance—sure enough, on the lighthouse's deck.

MIA

At eleven that night—with Britt about to sneak up to my window any minute so that we can find the next pages of the diary—there's a knock at my door. I shift on my window seat, tugging the curtains shut behind me in case she shows up.

"Come in." My voice cracks. *Shit. Get it together.*

Grams pokes her head in, brown eyes taking in my messy room, the makeup she wore at dinner scrubbed off her dark skin. "Hey." She steps inside, sliding the door closed behind her and nudging a bundled-up pair of sweatpants with her foot. "You got some cleaning to do tomorrow?"

I bite back a smile at the little things that stay the same, nodding, doing everything not to look over my shoulder. "Probably. What's up, Grams?"

Making her way across my floor, she sits on the end of my bed, resting her arms on her knees. "Your nana and I were just wondering how you were feeling? You were awfully quiet while the Garcias were here. Not so much giggling with you and Britt as usual."

Is this her way of asking about what Mom left me, about what I've found?

Maybe she really does want to know regardless of the pain, and I should just tell her. Maybe it would go better than I think.

"Grams," I whisper, testing the waters. "Do you think Mom had something to say?"

Her gaze shifts, always unfocused with the mention of her only daughter. She turns to my mirror, where a single rose sits—a gift from her and Nana after that middle school concert when diehard Tori Rose fans came with cameras and I decided I'd never be able to be myself beneath the spotlight. I'd only ever conjure an image, an echo of her and pain for everyone I love.

In that one gesture, I see how my grandmothers have fought through everything for my sake. It's forever evident in how Grams will never use this one pink mug in the cupboard but refuses to throw it out. It's in the way Nana will stand by the window for minutes on end, saying when asked if she's okay that she's listening for the sea. It's even clearer in how Grams would always hold my hand a second longer than necessary when she used to drop me off at school, and in the way Nana will study me when I'm not looking, like she's trying to find my mom in me—just as I always have, just like this town always has. I've seen every bit of hurt they've tried to shield me from, without them realizing that my *not knowing* her sometimes hurts worse than anything else.

"I don't know, Mia. But your mother always could say anything about everything, so I'm sure she would have found something to add." There's a wistfulness to it, but it never over-shadows that pain. I can't do this to her, to either of them. That's something that hasn't changed either.

They'll ask if they want to know. Maybe they really don't.

I get to my feet when there's a rustle at the window behind me.

I wrap my arms around her, curling my head into the nook of her neck like I used to when I was five and had a nightmare and she'd pick me up. She'd walk me around the house, rocking me, singing to me because even with all the tragedy it's brought us, music and storytelling still run in both our veins, as much as we fight it.

"I'm okay," I say. She needs to hear it, and I want her to be okay more than I want to be truthful. "I love you."

"I love you too." She takes a deep breath. "So much, baby."

Tears try to make their way out again hearing those words returned by one of the only two people who hasn't left me or planned to. I pull back because if we hug a second longer, I'll cry and she'll worry.

"Are you feeling okay about Britt leaving in a week?" she asks, not quite meeting my eyes, as if she knows what she'll find in them.

Think about it.

I blink hard. "I might head to bed, Grams. I'm feeling kind of tired."

She stands, stroking her thumb down my cheek. "Okay, love. I'm here if you need something. Sweet dreams."

"Goodnight," I say softly. She shuts the door behind her.

When she's gone, I rush to the window, shoving the journal into my purse, slinging it over my shoulder, and throwing open the curtains. Studying the firs beyond our lot, I can't find anyone. She's not here. My grip on the curtains loosens.

There's a soft knock on the window as Britt peeks out, bending over with laughter when I jump and then glare.

"Come on," she mouths, winking in response to the scowl I can't hold on to when looking her way.

I slide the window open, and I climb outside, all the while realizing that this one week to decide, to spend with Britt, could also be as close to my mom as I ever get. And as much as I need to find answers, I also need to make this chance, this opportunity to finally know Tori Rose, last.

Britt and I duck under caution tape into the lighthouse that radiates déjà vu. It's impossible to shake the drive here: a montage of my hair obscuring the view, Sunset Cove blurring past, and Britt constantly adjusting the radio, her hands never stopping their tap dance against the wheel.

Glancing around, neither of us speak aloud how all the songs we've written in this coastal tower have built a thick nostalgia in the air. The scents of perfume, sea salt, cheap vodka, and weed tickle my nose, from below, reminiscent of prom night.

"Do we open it?" Britt asks, looking around. "Your mom said what's in the envelope is for when we think we found the right place, right?"

I pull out the red envelope, tracing the clue, those lyrics I'll never listen to the same again. She said that once I've found the location to match the lyrics, I'll have instructions, and the instructions will lead me to the next pages. "Yeah. I think so." This has to be the place.

I open the lip of the envelope, careful not to make any tears. Rose-patterned stationery that carries the aromas of old books and floral perfume slips out, and my breath catches as I read aloud.

Mia,

So you're an adventurer too. Welcome to the first real clue. My mama (your grams) always told me I had a wild heart. She said never to tame it. I hope you never tame yours, love. Let it beat for you.

*I want to show you my project from when I was here.
I came back every now and then to visit my moms, and
it gave me something to do. I don't know if the person it
was meant for ever saw it, but I thought it might mean
something to you. I left my mark in memories.*

*You'll see what I mean. Find the initials I left. I
always did like people to know my name.*

There's more, but I stop there because instructions continue past that step.

Britt and I search for the initials together, scouring every inch of space that was featured in the video, sneaking out onto the deck into the cool ocean air. Stepping up onto the bottom bar of it, I lean slightly over, like that girl did in the clip. But my stomach drops and I can't do it. I can't get that close to falling.

When outside yields no results, we head back in, pull at the panels, peek behind the tarps, glance past the railing surrounding the lightless light into darkness—anything to see what propelled my mom to bring us here.

"Mia." Britt crouches where the edge of the floorboards meet the rail.

In front of her, tiny scratches over the corner of the floorboard are flushed in shadow. I grab my phone and illuminate them, revealing the inscription: *TR was here.*

Snap.

Dislodging a panel of planks, Britt reveals a large square hole, a couple feet in width and length.

"What the . . ." I scramble closer, helping her push it aside, our hands overlapping slightly as I peer down into nothing. "What do we do?"

Britt smiles at me with a softness that has this contrasting edge of its own. "When's the last time you said fuck caution?" She's already sliding through before I can respond, before I can wonder if she means that in more than this moment, if she's thinking of just earlier this night when I broke down after her set. Her landing echoes, and I follow. I leap as her words rattle our silence. I only hesitate a moment, but I know it spans forever between us.

With my landing, I stumble forward and she catches me, our arms meeting in the dark.

"Thanks," I say.

"Yeah," she says.

Her phone flashlight flickers on, and we break fully apart.

From what I can tell under its glow, stairs curl all the way down to the base of the lighthouse in these strange quarters. Burned-out candles line the steps, some of them so well-used they're puddles of wax on the floor. To our side are rows of pictures. It's a seemingly endless collage of Polaroid and printed, old and new, sun-bleached and forgotten.

Photos tinted at corners, nostalgia bleached by the sun.

Just like her song.

My attention is pulled to the very first one, starting off the stream of images before they become infinity, unraveling into the depths. There, between a group of girls in bikinis and sun hats, is a sign: Welcome to Sunset Cove, where dreams rise. Your journey starts here.

It can't be coincidence. *Your journey starts here.* It's the sign she focused on in the first pages of the diary.

Britt's staring at the same spot—she reaches around me to smooth the corner of the photo. "Read the next part," she says.

I do. She holds the phone up until my mother's words bleed into the light.

Here we are. Here you are. Are you ready? Deep breaths. I always did that. Before a gig (and eventually concerts), I'd take exactly twenty-seven deep breaths. I was never one for superstition, but fame makes you cling to the weirdest pieces of reality.

Your dad would do them with me. Those breathing exercises. When I walked into the lights and applause, he waited for me all the while.

Take a deep breath and follow the steps. Count out twenty-seven. Then you'll find me.

Love,
Mom

My heart hammers. My *dad*. She actually mentions him, talks about him in a way my grandmas won't and the media and people of this town aren't able to, since they don't know him either, despite all their speculation. She chooses to fill me in.

Beneath the eerie spark of the flashlight, slowly showing more of the pictures, this feels like a campfire story—as true as it isn't. My mother did this. She made this when she was here. And I will not mess this up like I do everything else.

It must have taken hours, days, weeks, years.

Far more time than I have.

Who was all of this for?

"It's like a time capsule," Britt says. "I wonder how we never knew about it. We've been here a million times." This was where we made slipup number six, fresh from the sea in early autumn and stealing each other's warmth.

I take another cautious step away from her. "Everyone likes secrets, I guess."

"A little too much." There's something in her tone I can't decipher.

But I don't try right now. We reach twenty-seven slowly, glancing at each other but not quite looking.

"Is this *Linnea*?" Britt pauses in front of an image of a young girl with black hair and a full smile, waving at the camera, laughing at something we can't see. It's undeniably Linnea, the owner of the Horizon—still the best diner in town, where we work part-time when I'm not at the inn and Britt hasn't got practice or things to do at Mrs. Garcia's art gallery. This is the second time Linnea has appeared in this hunt already. Should I hint at it, ask her about it, during my shift tomorrow?

My gaze trails over the next part of the wall. "*Britt.*"

She moves closer, and we look together.

Next to Linnea, one step down—exactly twenty-seven steps down from the top—is a picture of a teenage Tori Rose and a blond boy kissing her cheek. The image isn't of Patrick Rose, so this must be David Summers. They look so young, so happy. I step closer, tracing the edges of the print. I'm pretty sure Nana burned every picture of my dad the night he ran away from us.

Patrick or David? David or Patrick? Which of them is my father, if either?

Something bulges behind the photo. As Britt continues to scan the wall beside me, I dislodge a stack of papers, wrapped carefully in a plastic bag that's heavily duct-taped to the concrete wall, hidden by that picture.

I undo this makeshift cover to reveal her words, and I say, "It's here."

The first real clue, the continuation of those pages, what Patrick Rose asked my mom to wait for and how she left, all sit in my hands.

TORI

1989

David didn't look up when I crashed onto his floor through the window.

"Hey, T," he said. "Just felt like breaking and entering?"

"Doesn't count if you leave your window unlocked." Gesturing over my shoulder, I took him in. He sat in bed, reading Shakespeare, shirtless in his *Doctor Who* pajama pants. Outside, waves crashed.

"We'll call it a casual felony." He smirked and set the book down. "What's up?"

He studied me. I was still in my prom dress (a rose-patterned, scarlet contraption that I'd forced him to drive me to pick up).

All around his room, the walls were plastered with photos. I was in more than half of them, including the framed one by his bed of us biking along the shore. Me ahead, him pedaling to keep up. I still didn't know who took it.

"Tori?"

My eyes met his, and I sank onto the bed beside him. "You remember Patrick?"

"Mr. Fate?" He laughed. "From two hours ago?"

"Exactly." His book sat between us, and I played with the pages. I could do this with or without him. With him was always better for some reason. One day he'd stay and I'd go, but he could come. For now. I'd played it over ever since Patrick made his offer. It would work.

"What about him?" David asked.

"He's staying at the inn."

"Okay . . ."

"David, it *is* fate. It has to be. He asked me to go to Nashville with him. Music City. To become stars." The words rushed out. We'd been standing in the pale glow of the lobby's lamp. He'd talked so grand for a boy in beat-up sneakers and a devil-may-care grin. Something pulled me to him that was greater than myself. The universe. The music. Journey. *A* journey.

David's jaw literally dropped. "*What?*"

"He said he's going to make something of himself. He's going to go all in. He said I should come and we should sing like we did tonight."

Usually, David didn't question my ideas, no matter how wild. Jump off the bridge in the dead of night and see what it felt like to have the water catch us? No hesitation. Stand in the back of his friend Leah's truck bed and spread our arms to the wind to *fly*? We did it twice. This time, he pressed the tips of his fingers to his temples like his brain was combusting. "What if he's a murderer? You get in his car and—"

"I'm not driving with *him*." I turned away from the pictures the moonlight painted across his bare chest. I reminded myself only Tori Peters would focus on that. Tori Rose didn't. Not in the face of the music and it's far more plentiful possibilities.

David looked out the window I came through. "You get a car I don't know about?"

"I've got no future here. I've got nothing to lose," I pressed on.

"Except you know, you don't have a *car*. Would your moms even let you go?"

"Music is my dream. They understand that." They were the ones who bought me my guitar. Mama taught me how to tune it. Mom introduced me to Dolly Parton. They listened to every song I wrote.

"We did cover the possible murderer point, right?"

"Singing like that? David, there was something there. I *felt* it."

"Tori . . ."

"I want you to come."

"What?" That wasn't the word I was waiting for.

"Let's go together." I inched forward. "I've got savings from desk duty at the inn and my job from before. I can find work while I'm there too. It's our last summer . . ."

"It's our first summer together in years." His gaze dropped.

"First and last. Don't you want to make it great?" I took a deep breath. "I have an idea."

"Other than following some dude you just met?"

"I'm not following him. I'm following my calling. The universe is telling me to go."

"The universe has nothing on you."

"It has everything."

He sighed, giving in. "What's your idea?"

"We spend half the summer in Nashville. Then we go to New York and you see those theaters you've always wanted to see. Let's make it *our* Summer of Dreams." We could both get something out of it.

A beat of agonizing silence passed. He looked ahead at those frozen pictures of us.

"Okay," he said.

"Okay?" I squealed as quietly as I could (as to not wake his

parents and three younger siblings) and threw my arms around
him. He cleared his throat, patting my back in an uncharacteristically awkward way. I pulled back laughing.

His cheeks were flushed, and he glanced down at his lack of
shirt. *Oops.* "Yeah, okay, let's do it. Let's get out of here."

The anticipation, building nerves, and wanderlust calmed
with my next exhale. I slumped against his shoulder. I was *done*
waiting.

His hand rose, fingers trailing gently over the ends of my
hair, before he dropped it and picked his book back up. "You
staying?"

I'd already closed my eyes, falling into my own dreams.

My parents were harder to convince. The next morning, they
sat across from me at our kitchen table. Mama shook her head
as the request hung between us. Mom was silent beside her,
clicking her spoon against the edge of a cereal bowl. Her palm
rested against the stained wood, right over the spot where I'd
scratched my initials when I was seven.

"You want us to let you go across the country . . ." Mom
said. She held her hands up when I went to protest. "Just clar-
ifying. To make sure I'm hearing this right."

"Yes." The music hummed in every one of my veins, filling
them where blood should be.

"Tori," Mama said. "Sweetheart, this is . . . not entirely
thought out. Graduation is in a week."

"Yeah, I'd go after that." I leaned forward, foot tapping
against the hardwood. I had to go somewhere after grad. It was
the end of an era or something. "I want to see things. Do things."

"We know you do." Mama's eyes softened a little. I got my

drifter heart from her. She was the one who suggested she and Mom leave their town and make their own life.

"What if something goes wrong?" Mom's knuckles were white around her spoon.

"Then I'll figure it out. David's coming."

"Hold on. So now this is a cross-country trip with a boy?" *Two.*

"Yes. Because we're friends. Best friends."

They studied each other with another one of their telepathic stares. That same gentle nature was there whenever they met eyes. The same stare they had while whispering over morning coffee and singing to me before bed when I was young. The same as every time a romantic moment happened on the summer Sundays when we stayed up until midnight watching love stories on television. Like they saw people falling for each other and just had to meet eyes across the room, say with their gaze: *That's us. I found that feeling in you.*

They weren't married, but they were the truest example of love I'd seen. A love too pure and beautiful for vows of forever to be illegal.

And then the word fell from Mama's lips. "Okay."

Just like David had said the night before. That one word held every aspiration. It was the key.

"Really?"

"We're not going to hold you back. *But* there are going to be ground rules."

Mom nodded to that. "*Lots* of them. Starting with you calling us every night. No matter what."

"You have to stay to graduate."

"You need to plan out your trip and money with us before you go."

"And you need to know when to come home, baby," Mama said. "Don't get lost. Know you've always got a place here."

Both of them, almost in sync, extended their hands across the little table, and I wound my fingers around theirs.

"I will."

I could fit my way into most rhythms, but graduation was the exception. I'd barely scraped by, but here I was, peeking at David down the line and making faces. The move back to Sunset Cove threw things off, the music took my focus from work and essays, and I ditched school for it, finding this one hidden cove to curl up with my guitar. But today, it was over. Something new finally got to begin.

The crowd was too cheery and weepy, and I was vibrating with the image of Music City's lights and all I had to prove. I still took my time, never one to pass up a stage, but I got off as soon as my turn was over, waving to my moms and blowing a kiss.

After an eternity, David crossed too, and he found his way to me. His steps slowed and his grin started.

Gently flicking his tassel, I smiled. "Hey, congrats."

He wrapped his arms around me. "Congrats to you too, T." He held on a second, and I grinned into his shoulder.

Goodbye, high school. Good riddance.

"You ready to go?" I asked. "Patrick's meeting us by the sea."

"Ready as I'll ever be." He pulled back, and we left the caps falling like confetti.

Near the shore stood the boy with the rose tattoo. His smile gave his greetings and excitement away. His motive? Only fate could tell that.

"Hi," he said when we reached him, and his poet's eyes held mine.

"Hi." I stopped in front of him. A little too close. Just like when he'd asked me to come with him, that night, standing in front of the piano.

"Ready?" he asked, almost a whisper.

"Always," I said, nearly a shout.

We passed that taunting sign leading out of town, and I told David to stop. When he did, we scratched our initials into the post with a penny he found in his back pocket. And then the road became a blur. It was summer, squeezed into a collection of days. Laughter. Pit stops. Music. Dancing in the front seat. Street-lit parking lots where David ran in to get supplies while I hummed new Journey or Dolly Parton songs with Patrick Rose. Photoshoots with David who decided to bring a camera (to capture our dreams). Hasty meals and old record shops and more music.

Always, music.

David was a forever-reliable presence at my side through each moment. But Patrick was something new. Unfamiliar. And I caught myself looking too often at that tattoo with its delicate petals and thorns. A sign from the universe.

Patrick drove after us along the winding highways. David was in the driver's seat of his beat-up minivan, and I was next to him, but I was the one guiding us forward with a map unfurled on the dash. Strumming the guitar in my lap and whisper-singing songs I wrote, I thought of the boy trailing so close behind.

And one night, as another sunset kissed the horizon and lit us up in pink and gold, I saw the city for the first time. I saw the place I'd fallen asleep envisioning every night this week.

"Tori Rose," David said beside me, stalling so we could take it in. "Are you ready for a Summer of Dreams?"

"MEET ME
IN THE LYRICS"

From Tori Rose's debut solo album,
Forest in the Sea, *1991*

MIA

They let her go. They *let* her go. Passenger side in Britt's car, driving back through the night, I watch the beach homes and sandy stretches and strips of shops fly by. The lighthouse fades behind us while I flip through the envelopes in my purse. There are six to go and, as the dashboard clock changes to midnight, there are six days left until Britt and Lost Girls leave.

Britt's request for me to *think about it*, the look she gave me backstage just hours ago, is all I can hear or see even as she sits next to me.

It turns out my mother didn't run away like I'd thought for so long, inescapably entranced by the pull of her dream. She didn't just pick up and leave because of the music. She asked my grandmothers—her moms—and they let her go.

The pain in my grandmothers' eyes every day, the sadness they keep in, is it because they think it was their fault my mother left that final time, died away from them? That she didn't come home from that last tour? Is that why we don't talk about her? Do they regret that moment, regret that time they said *okay*?

Tapping my foot to "You All Over Me" playing from Britt's phone, I think of my mother leaving, of how the music called to her, and I wish I could forget everything for just a second. I wish I could remove the weight, the hurt I cause, and know who I am without it—know if that life could ever be meant for me. Because those first times, those first songs . . . In some ways it's the closest I've ever felt to her and the closest I've ever felt to me.

I'll be saying goodbye to more than Britt in six days.

Except . . . my grandmas *let* her go.

"Mia," Britt says, shattering our quiet.

I turn to where she sits, hands perfectly at ten and two instead of her arm leaning against the rolled-down window like usual. "You okay?"

"Are you?" She gives a short laugh when I don't reply. "I'm driving. I can't stare you down right now."

"I'm okay." I twist my fingers in my lap.

Britt nods, her mouth a thin line, and says, "I'm glad."

The drive across Sunset Cove is never quite long enough, and with those words, the inn's neon sign peeks through the homes and trees and streets. Still, she doesn't answer my question. She just keeps staring out at the road.

"I'm going to talk to Linnea during my shift tomorrow," I tell her, putting the envelopes away and tilting back against the leather headrest. "I think she knows something." I don't know if my mom told anyone else about the hunt, but Linnea has to be in it with intention. There's got to be a reason for all of this. She saved this so carefully, planned this so intricately.

"Okay." Britt nods.

"Do you have a shift too?" I smooth my thumb over the guitar ornament she's hung from the mirror. We usually work Saturdays together.

Pulling into the inn's parking lot, her tires crunch over gravel and her silver Honda—fondly nicknamed Dorothea—sways ever-so-gently from side to side over the uneven ground. "I'm not working there anymore. I talked to Linnea right before the party." She glances my way as if checking whether I'm still okay.

The Horizon without Britt is an image that doesn't quite compute. Then again, so is living in a town without her, listening to anyone else sing through all our monumental moments.

My hand drops to my lap. "Do you have practice?"

"One or two a day. We're going to hit it hard on the road and when we get there. But there's packing to do and . . . Oh shit, I forgot to pick up my dry cleaning."

"Dry cleaning?" I raise my eyebrows at her when she shifts into park. "Since when do you have dry cleaning to pick up?"

"I want to wear my lucky dress for our gig." She smiles, and my heart can't help fluttering at the memory.

Her lucky dress was what she wore to Lost Girls's first performance freshman year. She hit her growth spurt early in eighth grade and just never grew out of it. It's flowy, periwinkle, and what she was wearing right after slipup number three as well, underneath the bleachers at homecoming right after Lost Girls brought the stadium to their feet with the latest song we wrote. Nothing is quite as large a mutual turn-on as watching people fall in love with a song.

"We're here," Britt says when the silence lingers, and we both study each other a moment too long.

Six days.

I open the passenger door and swing my legs out, boots landing on the gravel. "Thanks for the ride. And the company."

"Thanks for the adventure." Britt smiles that ridiculously smug smile that makes something pull in my chest thinking of how she'd give me that look when she won a bet, stole a kiss, beat me at rock paper scissors for the last popsicle.

"Talk tomorrow?" My palm against the car door, something has me stooping down, still taking in the way the moonlight paints her, not closing it quite yet.

She nods, hands finally relaxing on the wheel and arm falling to lean against the side. "Tomorrow after practice. Maybe we can do some more looking then?"

"Do you need help packing?"

"Please, have you met Mile?" Rolling her eyes, she shakes her head, referring to her parents by their first names like she always does to avoid typical gender conformities. She's not wrong. Any inklings of type A Britt has are Mx. Garcia's handiwork.

"Bye, Britt." I almost reach out to squeeze her hand and she does the same, out of habit, but both of ours fall to our sides as if remembering another slipup isn't something we can take.

Her gaze is fierce, locked on mine still, but I know she's too proud to ask if I've made up my mind, and I'm too scared to answer. I break first this time, and my eyes return to the inn that's supposed to be my future, that *has been* my future ever since Tori Rose didn't come home.

I shut Britt's car door and turn my back, taking a deep breath. The gravel shifts again as she pulls out of the parking spot, and I look over my shoulder once, watching her taillights rejoin the streets of Sunset Cove, heading away from here.

And maybe it wasn't just my grandmas who let my mom go. Maybe this whole town did.

Linnea and I don't talk for the first hour of my shift. She's business first, motherly check-in later, and puts me to work right away. While she takes orders around the room, weaving between tables, I load the dishwasher. The eclectic nature of Sunset Cove accumulates in this diner with its checkerboard floor, hand-designed mosaic-topped tables, framed posters of celebrities including my mom, and the broken karaoke machine in the corner.

The words my mom wrote just for me whisper in my ear, and the orange envelope sits neatly folded in my large coat pocket as the song it's from plays on loop through the one earbud I have in. There's no time to waste. Mom is trying to tell me something, and I have under a week to hold her close and really listen.

I'm going to have to give Britt an answer, but I need the whole story first.

Tori Rose is the only one who's ever been willing to tell it to me, and in her lyrics, she continues.

When each song was over, your smile was on mine,
So don't forget it was the music, fate, that beckoned us
each time.
Meet me in the lyrics if you're brave, meet me in the
lyrics if you're true,
Just meet me in the lyrics so we can find our way back
to me and you.

There are so many places it could be, hidden in those words. This music video doesn't take place in Sunset Cove. It was filmed at the Bluebird Café in Nashville—practically just a live performance—but my mother had enough stage presence to make it feel like a show.

"Mia?" Linnea's voice comes from behind me, and she hits my arm gently with a rag. "I want to talk to you, kid."

"Mm-hmm?" I tug the earbud out, leaning back against the long counter, which, like the tables, has also been mosaicked. I heard from a classmate that the tiles in this diner were Linnea's own senior art project and that they've been here ever since, with a new table added by different grad classes for seven consecutive years and then no longer built upon, fading like traditions do.

"How are you doing?" She wrings the cloth between her hands. She's wearing her signature overalls that she carefully designs with various embroidered wildflowers. By now, she's in her late fifties, but I've only ever known her as quiet, tired, and older than her years, just from the way she surveys the room like she can see into everyone's hearts.

"I'm fine. How are you?" The envelope gets heavier in my pocket. I spent hours thinking of what to ask her until I fell asleep at three, still picturing Britt's smile.

I've always known Tori Rose in vignettes, unintentionally revealed. How she learned a whole Dolly Parton album the first day she got her guitar, how that guitar didn't used to have its signature roses on it, how she wrote her best songs in laughter, in midnight. The fragments of a fallen icon, a superstar or a girl.

What does Linnea know of that?

"Mia? *Mia?*" Linnea repeats.

I need to ask her something, anything to get this conversation started.

"Sorry, what?" I shake my head, facing her, steadying myself.

"Are you doing all right? You seem off." Her lips tip up, sad, cautious. "So I guess you've heard Britt's heading out early?"

Why do people only ever want to talk about heartbreak? *No*, not heartbreak. After all, Britt's doing what she's always dreamed. That counts for everything no matter what words I have to eventually say.

"I . . ." I take a step back and pick up a rag of my own. "Linnea, how did my mom die?"

It comes out a whisper, but I may as well have yelled it for how her face falls completely. *Shit.* I almost reach forward and hug her, tell her she doesn't have to answer that.

"Well, that was unexpected." Linnea whistles low.

"I'm sorry."

"Don't be, kiddo. By the way, I wanted to run something by you."

Is she avoiding the question? Ignoring it completely? By-passing another story like this town always does in the name of Tori Rose's glory, her fame?

Linnea keeps going, pushing past it, and part of me wants to bring out the envelope, leave, and go find more on my own. But she says, "I thought you might want to know, I've decided to fix up the karaoke machine. Maybe get those Friday night open mics up and running again." There's a softness to her gaze and remembrance in her eyes as she smiles in the direction of the creaking stage. "Might be time."

I don't breathe, just let it settle. "Linnea, I . . ."

She's lost in the thought. "I guess bringing back some of the everyday Tori never hurts. God, that girl's got records and monuments to remember her."

I open my mouth again, ready to interject, to try again, and possibly even share a piece of the truth with her, but no words come out. *Monuments.*

That's it.

"I think that's a great idea," I say in a rush, and she smiles, placing a hand on my arm briefly before straightening her apron, walking away without finishing our conversations. I'm already clicking *call* on my phone. Asking Linnea any more questions will have to wait for now.

Just when I think it's going to voicemail she answers. "Hey, hey, just got out of practice. What's up?"

"I know where the next clue leads."

MIA

Britt parks outside Back to Me & You, and I get out, standing next to her in front of my mother's tribute club. The walls are pink and the roof is glass, lit by the waning sky. This place is open from sunset to sunrise, and the parking lot is filled with cars and motorcycles, but everyone's already inside.

Listening to that song in the Horizon and reading the clue, I just assumed it was between the lines and history, like with the lighthouse. Not right there in the lyrics.

Meet me in the lyrics so we can find our way back to me and you.

And here we are, at this club that's twenty years young and shining in the dark. It's an actual monument to who she was, a haven that her music made with a little less tourism and superficiality than the rest of the town. At least here—unlike the pub on Main Street—they don't serve a drink called the Tori Rosé.

Crossing the lot, Britt and I head for the entrance covered almost completely by torn-off ticket stubs from Tori Rose concerts. I hold the door for Britt, and she slips in, her sparkly red cardigan brilliant in the sea of the crowd. I step inside next, smoothing my hands over my leather skirt that kind of matches the one on the poster of my mother's *Regret You* tour—her final album—and doesn't quite seem to match me.

My mom's voice plays over the speakers, the same song my grandmas danced to at their wedding ten summers ago. "Remember Me."

How does remembering work if it lets you forget me?
How does forgetting work if when I think of you, I can't
breathe?
But I wouldn't change these memories, no matter where
we go,
Because loving you was the best part of me I ever got to
show.

I spent every weekend at Back to Me & You before it went full-on nightclub under new ownership. I used to bike across town, sit out front, and ask anyone who'd listen about my mom. But I got those same half-hearted answers: superstar, legend, great style, good hair, that *voice*.

Peeking over her shoulder, Britt mouths, "*Coming?*" She catches the spotlight like we tried to catch butterflies in our youth, flying even when she lands in its trap.

And yet I follow her.

Bodies rustle through open space, and sequined dresses and tailored pantsuits slip by us. People carry instruments past the stage twice as large as the Horizon's and equipped with a working spotlight. Britt and I find a table in the back, between a couple tuning guitars and a group of Sunset Cove Community College students crowded around a menu: my future.

Next year, I'll stop my ping-ponging between the Horizon and the inn, no longer having my own little escape at the diner, and work with my grandmas full time. I'll attend Sunset Cove Community College, and that'll be it. I avoid that group's gaze and general direction, bringing a few too many looks from Sunset Cove passersby.

I still have time.

"Hey." Britt smirks across the table.

"Hey." My pulse pounds, and I look around as music and laughter rise. "How was practice? How's Lost Girls?"

Her whole expression comes to life with the question. "It's great. If Amy and I can just agree on the last song for the set-list, then we've got it. That'll be the gig."

"What are the choices?" I spent the time between what little sleep I got last night and brainstorming questions to ask Linnea watching and rewatching that latest video Britt posted on her channel. I memorized every word she wrote about a girl who chased the sun and fell for the rain. It goes along to a softer track I left on her nightstand, twinkling piano between minor chords, *Chords by Mia Peters*, written with a purple heart in the description.

"'How to Say Goodbye' and 'Heart-Shaped Looking Glass.' Amy thinks 'Heart-Shaped Looking Glass' goes with the fairy-tale theme, but I think we need something different, something to mix it up."

"What does Sophie think?"

"Sophie thinks we should add a larger piano solo to both." Britt laughs. "Then she'll choose."

"I agree with you." My mother always did just what Britt is suggesting. She set the tone of the album, but there was this one song that spoke to something unexpected, twisted the rest of it on its head, and made the whole work have a new lens. The next words come out quieter, and I wish I could snatch them back as soon as they're gone. "I'm always on your side."

There's this one variation of her smile that she saves just

for me. It's a little like a whispered secret, a sacred oath. "Oh yeah? I wish you could vote then."

There's a pause, heavy as it is long, and we avoid one another's gaze as the words rest between us. There *is* a way I could vote. If I did more than write tracks and watch practices, if I wasn't so scared, if me getting up on a stage didn't remind everyone of what exactly the world lost when it lost Tori Rose.

But I still *can't*. Am I fooling myself thinking there's really a decision to make? Hasn't it already been made?

"I'm going to go get drinks." Britt pushes back from the table when I can't find the words to say.

"Drinks," I agree. I spin the saltshaker with one hand, keeping my eyes on its guitar shape and not her. "Sounds good."

I want you to come.

As soon as her heels clip away, I look up and watch her leave. I watch her flipping her fake ID between her fingers as she makes her way to the bar. There are just enough out-of-towners for her to slip through unrecognized. She doesn't drink often, only at parties or after she aces finals—when the two of us sneak some liquor from Nana's stash and replace it with water—but whenever she does, she can work a fake ID like no one else. We got ours together last summer.

I pull the orange envelope from my purse. I have to find my mother's message and what it means for me. I have to assume it'll show me what to do without hurting any of the people I care about.

I place the envelope on the table next to the salt and pepper. I study my mom's handwriting, and I don't know how to get used to seeing the way she so carefully writes my name when nothing else about her was careful. My breath shudders on the way out.

"What should I do?" I whisper.

The envelope stares back, the letters swaying in and out of focus as I blink.

A waitress I don't recognize makes her way over. Her name tag reads "Owner (she/her)," without a name. She pauses a second, balancing a tray of used glasses and empty plates. "Can I get you anything?" Her eyes are on the envelope, and I almost tuck it away.

Her hair is a light purple, close to white. Freckles dot her pale nose and cheeks, and her eyes are endlessly blue. She looks to be in her late forties or early fifties, close to Linnea's age. Her makeup is flawless. She must be the one who turned this place into a club—the *owner*.

"No, thank you," I say, still staring at that word clipped to her shirt collar. "My friend is getting drinks."

She's staring in return. "Do you come here often?"

"No." Not now.

But she doesn't move on. She stands there and tries to place me before her mouth forms a perfect O, the shape peoples' mouths usually make when they realize. Her gaze locks on the poster I didn't realize was behind me. It's the *Regret You* deluxe album cover in which half my mom's face is photographed—wig red and wild—and the other half is made of a rosebush with only thorns.

"You're . . ." There's something in her eyes and it hits me all at once. There's something beyond just recognition. "You're her kid, aren't you?"

"Mia. I'm Mia Peters." It's clear from the lines of her features, the downturn of her lips, the way she's looking at the clue on the table, there's something new I haven't seen before.

Britt moves into view, two glasses in hand. Her eyes dart between me and this woman and my mom's legacy somewhere in between. The owner is staring with greater intensity, and my stomach flips.

"What's up?" Britt slides onto my side of the booth, putting herself between me and this woman.

"Nothing," I say.

The owner shifts, purple hair falling off her shoulders.

Britt doesn't believe me. "Hi," she says, her tone curt in a way I haven't heard before. "I'm Britt."

Gesturing to her name tag, even with its lack of name, the owner shakes her head. She leaves as suddenly as she came. I want to get up, but my feet are stilled. I will them to move, to follow, but I'm left staring after this person who *owns* this club dedicated to my mom. Just as I'm about to push myself forward, Britt slides the glass my way.

"That was weird," she says. "The bar was so busy tonight. The guy didn't even card me. Who was that?"

"I don't know. She knows my mom."

"*Knows* knows her?" She pauses midsip.

"I think so."

There was something in the way she looked at the envelope. I grasp it tighter.

My mom had to have sent me here for a reason.

I don't say anything else, and Britt's gaze is locked on the crowd. My breath is still uneven as I open the letter, sitting beneath my mother's songs, pouring from all directions as I read.

Mia,

Welcome to the place the sun sets latest. Everyone knew my ego didn't need the added boost of this tribute, but I'm glad you're here. I wanted you to meet someone very important to me.

You'll probably find her at the bar. Tell her me and the music say hi. She'll lead you to the next parts of our story. She'll know what I mean.

Love,
Mom

It is her. It has to be. I stare after her purple hair, barely visible as she retreats. Then the owner ascends the rectangular stage at the front of the diner—to the left of the bar—under the blinking skylight and decals of budding roses on the walls.

"Who wants to sing?" she asks the bar's crowd with surprising enthusiasm. I half expect her to belt out the words to one of my mother's hit tunes. "Rules of open mics at Back to Me & You are simple. I'll call you up, you get your ass on stage, and we never boo anyone unless they really deserve it."

There's a quick chuckle. Britt and I get up, making our way through the crowd and toward her. This woman has to be who my mother was talking about.

"Do we have any volunteers?" she calls.

Britt raises her hand. She's always ready for the music.

But then she turns to me. "One song?" she asks, hand still raised. "Sing with me."

One song. After all this time, can't I give her just one song? I haven't sung since that show.

There was a time we sang together for people, when that was our thing and our songs were just ours. All those years ago, my mom got up on a stage to make fate happen for herself. Shouldn't I try? If there's anywhere in Sunset Cove that might be safe to, it's here where her person is honored with her story. It's here where she's led me. It's here with Britt.

The woman on the stage points to Britt through the crowd, and I grab Britt's hand, squeeze it yes. Her smile lights up my world, and she raises our interlocked hands into the air.

I can do this. *I can do this.*

For Britt. For Tori Rose.

Face falling when she sees me with Britt, the owner slowly lowers the arm she's pointing with, but it's too late. We're making our way through the crowd.

"And who are you?" she asks in this practiced way, into the mic.

"Britt Garcia." Britt's glowing. She's so beautiful. She shines. These are the times we slip up, because how is it possible to not want to kiss her when she looks that alive?

"Mia Peters," I whisper, hoping it's swallowed by the noise.

Cheers echo, knowing me as they always do from name and appearance. My mom was Tori Peters before she was Tori Rose, and apparently that was exactly who she left Sunset Cove to escape. With my grandmothers' permission.

But this is one more chance to sing with Britt before she leaves after a lifetime of whispered and exchanged melodies. Six days is turning to five, and her goodbye aches a little less with the promise of a song.

People are calling us up to that stage, and Britt's hand is still tangled with mine. I should take every moment I can get—plus, the owner is already up there. Trailing after Britt, a step behind, I weave through the parting crowd, toward the mic. But, too soon, I look behind me, and my own eyes reflect back to me through my mom's portrait in a nearby window.

"Ready?" Britt shouts over the claps, turning back under the flush of the skylight.

Phone flashlights flicker, swaying to nonexistent music, cameras rise, and that picture stares, my mother's blue eyes seeing everything.

It's too late.

I've played Spot the Difference too many times and fought for similarities, but there are so many more differences, and looking her in her daring eyes only confirms that.

I'm moving away, peering at that poster, and finally knowing who I am as the crowd presses in. This club is a tribute to who my mom was. The people here remember her the best of anyone in this town, better than any of the half-drunk partiers at graduation or people in the inn or the Horizon. This whole club represents the legend I'll never live up to.

The journal is everything—it's already shown me part of who she really was—but I also know from my own intentions for this summer and her words that I *am not her*. I have the angles of her features when I search for them, I have her songs in my heart, but I will never have her fate, and I will never get out of this town.

So I run like I always do, but for the first time, it's away from Britt, pushing through the door and into the chilly night. When there's nowhere to go, I sit on the curb, gasping for air. The parking lot is silent, and I wonder momentarily if Britt's going to come. *Please don't let her come.* When I look back, she's already taken the stage, scanning the room, still searching for me in a way that I hope she one day—in six-almost-five days— won't, if only so I can stop being the person who lets her down.

I bury my face in my hands.

It's a couple cold minutes of sitting on the curb with the orange envelope at my side before the door opens behind me and a song in Britt's voice—"How to Say Goodbye"—spills out. Silver boots stop next to me, and my eyes travel to the face of their wearer, who scuttles away like a deer in headlights.

"Wait!" My voice cracks, and I stand again. "Wait. Please." The owner of Back to Me & You's focus whips toward me as she slides into the driver's seat of a black sports car that makes me think of funerals and goodbyes. "Please."

It's a staring contest.

The two of us stand there.

Me: wobbling on heels in a tank top and skirt that are now too tight, outside another place that immortalizes my mother.

Her: in her car, with answers I need as badly as air. Her,

shaking her head before she turns the key in the ignition, leaving me shivering in the parking lot and feeling like I'm going to lose everything in my stomach.

"Wait," I say to no one as she pulls onto the road beneath red taillights and the twilight sky.

The wind slaps me, and the keys around my neck are freezing my skin. I can't go back in; I can't leave; I can't stay.

I can't do anything.

I can't do nothing, so I pull them off, taking the mystery key in my hand as I wind around the side of the building. I pull off my heels, feet throbbing, careful not to step on the shattered glass littering the ground in multicolored shards. There are five doors, and I try my odd key in them all like I sometimes will. Back here, the music is finally silent, and I'm at peace.

The key doesn't even slip inside the first door like I knew it wouldn't. It never does, but I keep going, clearing my head, fighting for control. The second fits, but it won't turn. The third and the fourth are the same, and breathing gets a little easier, a little slower. One more. Deep breath.

I slip it in, and the fifth door is different. For a moment, I believe I'm high on the music, on the longing, but the key undeniably slips into the lock, turns, and lets me inside.

MIA

After months of trying the key from that forgotten house by the shore in every odd door I come across, it lets me into a storage room. Pink twinkle lights line the ceiling, so close together they practically make one slab, and a dim light is cast across the objects of the room.

Cold sweeps over me, and I prop the door open with an empty beer box left behind the building.

Boxes, records, CDs, and instruments long past their golden years litter the floor, not too different from the west side of the inn. The walls are plastered with posters of Fate's Travelers. My mother's former band consists of five members: a pianist with ebony braids and dark skin—music prodigy Sara Ellis; a pale purple-haired lead guitarist . . .

Edie Davis.

That's who she was. That's who owns this place. Behind the crow's feet in the corners of her eyes and dark circles beneath them, I should've known. I should've seen the clues in her aged features, but most of my searching has been for Tori Rose alone.

And what is Edie Davis doing in Sunset Cove? She wasn't

born here, was never reported to live here. The only connection she supposedly has to our town is a prior partnership, maybe friendship, with my mom.

Continuing to scan the posters, I note the rest: a drummer with olive skin and midnight hair—Mateo Ramirez; a boy with a tan and brown curls that fall to his shoulders—Patrick Rose from the diary; and my mother. My mom stands back-to-back with Sara, arms crossed and laughter in her blue eyes.

Along the other side of the room are everyday pictures. There are Polaroids of her holding hands with a blurred figure, and they form a collage like the one below the lighthouse. Right underneath them is a verse from "Remember Me." I take a step forward, stumbling over another box, and my eyes fall on the last poster, spread across the wall in front of me.

It's framed with a gold record at the bottom. The image is of my mother, her hair in midwhip, her sequined dress spinning around her legs, and her microphone thrust into the air like she's asking the crowd to sing. I did that once, alone in my bedroom in front of my mirror, pretending I was her.

The poster reads: Tori Rose—2006—*Regret You* Tour.

That last tour, the one she never came home from. I take another step toward it, reaching for it.

"Mia?" Britt's voice is near, off the stage. "Mia? What was that? Where are you? Why did . . ." She trails off as the door slips open, and she steps in too. "What the . . ."

She's not looking at me. She's studying the room, shaking her head as her hand finds mine. Every now and then, her fingers tap absent-minded melodies along my skin, and tonight they ghost "Remember Me" across my palm in an unspoken comfort.

"I think I just need to take this week for what it is," Britt says finally. *Goodbye* is the clarification she doesn't add, and I swallow.

It sounds like she's giving up on me. Finally.

She continues. "People *know* your name, Mia. And God, I want that. I want that so bad. They want to hear you sing before you even open your mouth. But music isn't something for the scared."

I breathe in, face her, and I take her other hand. "You're right. I'm so sorry I couldn't even give you a song. I . . . I wanted to." I can't make more words come after the confession, so I just hold on as long as I can before we both need to let go.

She gently lifts the key around my neck, and it catches the light. "You found the door."

"The key worked."

"I assumed. I wonder . . ."

"Yeah?"

She disentangles our arms and steps around me, tapping the corner of that poster. Her slightly bitten nail pokes the frame, and I follow where she points at the diary pages shoved and pressed behind the glass.

We move toward them, sliding the poster off the wall. Together we undo the clasps pinning the back of the frame, lift the page, and unearth the papers pressed beneath it.

TORI

1989

The first day of the rest of my life began with a song. My own, of course. In the passenger seat of David's car, my fingers settled against frets as the hour slid past midnight. I found melodies begging to be heard as we entered the place where dreams really *did* rise.

I leaned as far forward as I could with my guitar in my lap, and I felt the sense of place in my bones. Calling me.

Music City was a city disguised as a town: lit up and neon and burning bright. The streets were quieter than I thought, but there was an energy to them that Sunset Cove could never match. People sporting instruments like mine made their way out of shops and across the streets. In the dark, they glowed. With ambition. With promise. With music. The signs along the road flickered. A rainbow of sights and sounds.

Someone waved to me, and I rolled the window down to wave back, which had David grinning. Music Row glimmered beneath the moonlight. Centennial Park flashed under street-lights. We drove like we were trying to discover every secret the city held before we even thought to stop at a hotel. This place was *something* waiting to happen.

I was going to make something happen.

"Is it everything you imagined?" There was an unusual note in David's voice I couldn't quite place.

"*Yes.*"

Sunrise painted the sky. We had only just parked when the lull of dawn had us drifting off. We found a rundown place about twenty minutes away from East Nashville (music and art burst from the seams there).

Patrick met us on the curb. The way his eyes met mine told me he felt the same way I did upon stepping foot on these streets. Lyrics radiated from him, and I pulled him forward, slipping my hand into his. We walked into this dream he'd spoken of together as David opened the door to the hotel.

The place was worn-out and as cheap as we could find. The lobby was filled with cracking drywall, stained carpets, and an old desk that took up more space than there was to stand. Somehow, it was perfect.

A man in a pinstriped vest sat behind the counter, flipping through a book. I couldn't see the cover. "Can I help you?" he asked before we reached the desk.

The wheels of our suitcases thudded behind us. Stars covered the walls like back in the Horizon. But it was different. It meant something here.

"We'd like to check in." I took the lead, rifling through my pink purse, catching David's eyes. "Is it cheaper if we share?"

He shrugged. "Probably."

"Yes," the man said without looking up from the page he was reading.

Patrick glanced between the two of us as he paid for his own room.

I swapped savings for freedom and a silver hotel key.

"Race you." I smirked at David and Patrick, and I didn't wait for a reply. Through the plain walls and faux crystal chandeliers, I ran. The hotel was only two floors, and the elevator had an out-of-order sign that seemed more a permanent fixture than a warning. So we took the stairs, and I laughed as we stumbled.

On the rectangular second story, we traced fingers across silver numbers on doors, matching our keys to the markings. And then there they were, 4B and 7B, right across the hall from one another. I placed my hand on the knob of the first.

"Find something to eat after we settle in?" I asked Patrick.

He nodded, tossing a quick smile my way and disappearing.

David and I slipped inside. The room was small and beige with one dresser, a window leading out to a rickety iron balcony, a tapestry of a daisy on the wall, and one bed.

"We're here," David said. His blond hair was tousled. His green eyes were bright.

"We're *here*." I flopped onto the bed, nearest to the window. "This is my side."

His cheeks flushed, and I rolled my eyes. We'd shared a bed before and a sleeping bag one year at summer camp when guys in his cabin pranked him with ants in his. Just that week I'd woken up with my head on his shoulder. But I got it, in a way. This was different. Nashville was a place of possibilities.

I hopped to my feet.

We unpacked a little while I hummed, and he smiled again. There was a sweeping nature to our movements as we unloaded our things, but I could never sit or stand still. I gave up halfway through my suitcase and headed to the window. Shoving it open, slinging my leg through, and climbing outside into this night, I breathed in deep. The balcony swayed beneath me as I stared at Nashville and the constellations that crowned it. I leaned on the rail, looking at how Music City shined.

With a creak from behind me, David joined. His fingertips grazed the small of my back as he found his footing. The hem of his bright-red T-shirt fluttered in the breeze.

"Thank you," I whispered without looking at him.

"For what?"

"For taking me to my dreams."

He stood there a second with his mouth gaping. His lips tipped up just slightly, and he turned his cheek before he met my eyes again.

"Sure thing," he said.

"What are you going to do here?"

"Write a play."

"Really? David, that's amazing. What about?"

He winked. "I'll tell you soon." And he left it at that.

Giving him a small smile, I moved back toward the window, which he'd propped open with his shoe (I had barely noticed he was half-barefoot). "I've got to call my parents."

"Tell them I say hi." He looked out at the city, arms resting against the rail.

Inside, I picked up the phone, dialed the number, and listened to it ring. As I waited, I forced myself to look away from the stardust that caught on David's silhouette.

"Mom? Mama?" I whispered, cradling it to my ear. Butterflies erupted inside my chest, and I welcomed them. "I'm *here*."

David stayed out on the balcony watching the city for way longer than I had the patience for, so I crossed the hall in my unicorn slippers, blouse, and jeans to knock on Patrick Rose's door.

It swung open after the first knock, and he leaned against it. "Hi, Tori Rose." He brushed loose ringlets out of his face, and I had the urge to weave my fingers into his hair.

"Hi, Patrick Rose." I let myself inside.

If it weren't for David and his surprising cleanliness, my hotel room would probably look like this too. Guitar set safely on its own chair. Clothes everywhere. Shoes kicked off halfway across the floor.

He nudged a loose pair of socks, slightly sheepish. "Sorry for the mess."

I sat next to Cash on the well-loved green armchair, tracing over a small dent in the otherwise smooth red wood. "Lucky for you, I thrive in dysfunction."

"That is lucky for me." He leaned against the wall. "So what brings you here?"

"I want to figure out what's next."

I wanted to get started on our dreams.

"I . . ." Patrick shifted from foot to foot. "Just first . . . You and David . . . are you together?" He looked back at his door like he could see our room through it. This wasn't what I meant.

"Nope."

"I just thought . . ."

I shook my head. Smiled. "You thought wrong."

We were almost together for a moment, that one day when David and I kissed, but I told him it was a mistake and we couldn't do it again if I wanted to keep my heart wandering. David was Tori Peters's love. He was Sunset Cove's golden boy. He was a piece of my past. Before the stage name became me and the music encompassed the only soulmate that could keep me. Best friend or not, David remained the one thing here tying me to that town. I wanted him here but not *that* way.

The fate-made boy with the rose tattoo didn't look quite convinced, but he tried to act it.

I took another step forward, closer than ever. I leaned in and said, "There's nothing there. Not with him. What about you, mystery boy? You got someone back home?"

He shook his head, and he only had eyes for me. "No." It was a breathless whisper.

I asked again, "What's next?"

His gaze fell from mine to my mouth, and that devil-may-care grin came back again.

Music City knew how to party. I'd thought I did too. I was the life of every party back in Sunset Cove. Dancing on tables. Drinking whatever I could find. Kissing strangers. Flirting with girls over drinks. Winking at guys before I walked out of the room. Getting drunk off life and something else. But *this*. This was new.

Country had taken over the basement of an artsy place near Music Row, filled to the brim with life and people. Guitars were in laps. Couples draped over each other in corners and at the bar. It was covered in spotlight, and I was alight under it. Everyone was.

David hung back near the door, finding a quiet corner to settle in such an uncharacteristically subdued way.

"*You okay?*" I mouthed.

He nodded and gave a thumbs up. When he took out a notebook, I let him be.

It didn't take long for Patrick and me to weave our way into the crowd. I barely knew him, but that was part of the excitement. It was part of the magic in the way we melded into each other's beats.

We slipped into a group near our age at the back, talking about how the music got them.

Edie Davis. A pale, purple-haired girl with a leather jacket, leaning against a sofa that was tainted with whiskey. She spoke of her first rock band and kissing a girl after church who made her want to play love songs.

Sara Ellis. A Black girl with braids draped over her shoulder, sliding up sunglasses that caught the spotlight as she raised her cup to take another drink. She was a piano prodigy who'd been converted to country by its storytelling.

Mateo Ramirez. A boy with an olive complexion and a tipped party hat resting on his head who grew up in Music City with the melodies always in his veins. He was sharing a chair with Sara, who had her legs swung over his lap as she balanced her glass on her knee. He tapped two drumsticks he'd called Dungeons and Dragons against the side table.

Sara glanced at us as we arrived. She didn't say hi. Didn't request our names. Just said, "How did the music get you?"

It wasn't clear how it happened, but somewhere between shots and chatter, at that party, a band was formed. Sara, Mateo, Edie, Patrick, and me. We called ourselves Fate's Travelers. We practiced in the unused event room of Patrick's and my hotel. Covered a thousand songs. Learned to build off the rhythms of each other's hearts.

But we were missing something important.

It was midnight, hunched over some sheet music as Sara riffed on the piano, when she and I decided what.

"CHASING SUNSETS"

From Tori Rose's 1992 sophomore album,
Bittersweet Beginnings

MIA

The first day of the rest of my life began with a song.

I lie across the Garcias' living room couch, just as at home in their purple cottage—nearly as close to the sea as you can get—as I am in my own. Maybe more. As much as the guilt fills me when I think it, their house feels full, happy, *whole*. The cool salt of the ocean hangs in the air, weaving through the glass doors, mixing with acrylic paint and a hint of perfume.

Britt's always told me that in her family wanderlust is a hereditary trait, that she was born with her eyes on the horizon, on something else—something great. Even just the photos on their walls show that, highlighting that perpetual look in her eyes.

While she finds rhythms along the piano, her parents weave around the kitchen, dishes clattering to a tune of their own. They sneak glances at us, smiling.

I turn onto my side, resting my head in the crook of my arm as I watch how Britt sits, back straight, arms relaxed, making the music sweep over the room. Behind her, still frames are displayed like she's got her own version of the legends on the

Horizon's walls. There are oil paintings similar to what Mrs. Garcia showcases in her gallery and photos of Britt's life: her and her cousins at la Feria de Cali, her first bike, her first show, even one of the two of us as toddlers sitting with a ukulele in her bedroom. She grows up with each one.

"Britt?" It comes out so quiet, I'm not sure she hears.

But she does. "Yeah, Mi?"

Her cardigan shimmers in the dimmed light of the chandelier, and my black skirt swallows any glow that lands my way, any spotlight that illuminates me. Like an omen, like another of the signs my mother writes of.

Atop the fireplace, a Garcia family portrait sits, preserved in laughter.

"How are you feeling about Nashville?"

It's not often I startle her, we're so attuned to one another by now, but she spins to face me. "What?" The dance we've been doing to avoid this topic falters, but I need to know that she's okay too.

"Nashville, the place, doing this for real. Leaving. Do you want to talk about it?"

Her eyes flicker away from the keys—to me. "Do I want to talk about it? Mia, I've been doing everything to not talk about it."

I bite my lip, hating that I made her feel like that. "I thought maybe when you're a star, I could come watch your shows. Cheer you on." The music may not be for me, I may not be able to be hers, but maybe this doesn't have to be forever. Whoever my father is still watched my mother's solo shows, taking those breaths with her backstage, watching her shine. I don't know if I can handle another goodbye for good.

A sad smile slips across her features. "You're the first person I want to cheer with."

With.

"But you don't have to." She turns away. "I don't need you to feel that hurt just to come see me."

"I always want to see you." It's the closest to the truth I've come. I imagine seeing her every day, going with her.

And then there's the flashing lights, Tori Rose's name on everyone's lips. All over again, I'm not enough like her and yet too similar, forever reminding everyone. Reminding myself.

Britt's gaze tracks the sky beyond the window, and she says, "I guess I'm nervous. It's new and just look how your mom describes it."

"A jump from Sunset Cove." I sit up, resting my arms on my knees.

"The biggest," she whispers. "It's where I want to go. It's what I want to do. But I'm nervous and tired of the expectations here, the ones that will come there. I'm tired of people who think they get gold stars for fulfilling what they believe to be some limited diversity quota or shit like that. When I get to Nashville, I just want to sing."

She inhales roughly, and I stand, step forward, sit beside her now. Her arm brushes mine, and her fingers trace C sharp.

I nudge her, face her, say, "Sing here. Now. Whatever you want."

There's a pause as the tracing of her nail along the ivories stops and her shoulders relax with the request of the music. She closes her eyes, and I hear before I see the motions of her hands—the song they capture in their voyage. I recognize it instantly.

"Loveless Stars."

My breath catches with this goodbye song at her fingertips. Her voice is low, mesmerizing, soft in my ear.

There's something calling me from you, calling me away,
But darling we knew when we began this love, I never
*   really stayed.*
I told you my heart retired early, my heart followed itself
*   home,*
And for you and me, there was never reason to build
*   our own.*
The memories come unraveled, goodbye's only a word,
We're just a wannabe broken heart, split between two girls.

Her voice cracks on the *broken heart*, and I'm rooted in place by her tone, by the way each word lingers.

So in the shadows of my heartache, I find myself anew.
Don't apologize any longer for just not loving you,
And when these loveless stars wink out
Betrayal is written across the sky.
I hope you know the best thing I can do for you is say
*   a quick goodbye.*
When these loveless stars wink out, when it's our turn to fly,
I hope you know the constellations were never built to
*   survive.*
Through supernovas and lost light and a broken,
*   shining path,*
They whisper their true intentions, poets so long as
*   they last.*

The second verse comes, and I listen as she commands the moment, as she sings her heart out here.

When you ask me why, when you say to stay,
I'm going to tell you it's better off this way,

*Better off with midnight kisses that never lingered to
    dawn,*
Better off with late-night chatter, come sunrise all gone,
*Better off with no hearts on sleeves, for mine's caged
    inside,*
Better off without the truth, for there's safety in our lies.

Her voice grows stronger when she's ready for it to, and every note to leave her lips hangs suspended in time and what little space there is between us. She takes the song to its end. The piano finishes, her voice stops, and she's left breathless and staring at the keys. We're both left breathless as I stare at her.

She pushes back from the piano, and the bench shifts while she gets to her feet. The pull of her, *her* gravity is impossible to resist.

We learned in science sophomore year it's rare for stars to exist alone. Most are at least in pairs, binary stars that circle each other in their movements. That's her and the music—here, now— but I think, for one glittering moment, that's what we were too.

That moment is over, but still, that doesn't stop me from wasting all my wishes on her. It doesn't stop the fact that, watching her here, I think I've only ever had feelings for her. I don't know how to need another person who'll leave, but despite trying so hard to save my heart, I don't know how not to be pulled in when she sings like that.

"Let me ask you something." Her breathing is heavy, and she steps closer, resting her hands on my shoulders.

I tilt my chin up, and we're shielded by the curtains of our hair, by this night, on the piano bench in her living room. "Any-thing." *Just don't ask me to go again. Don't ask me for the music. Don't make me let you down.*

"What do you *want* your mom's hunt to say?" She crouches

so we're closer to eye level, and how can I both want to kiss her and want to *not* want it this bad?

I close my eyes, and I'm honest. "I want a sign."

She pulls back, but the intensity of her stare doesn't lessen. She gives me the same look she'd give when she shook me awake to quiz her one more time for finals and then swatted me with the pillow I threw at her face until I caved. She looks at me like she always does. Like she doesn't want to let go.

"Okay." She nods slowly. "So let's find one."

I leave a note with chords on Britt's bedside table and, for once, I don't escape through the window. With Lost Girls bound to arrive for her early morning practice any minute now, I fling my denim jacket over my pajamas. I steal one last look at her curled into her pillow, lips slightly parted as she sleeps, before I head downstairs.

I reach the base of the stairwell and the vase of lavender on the entry table, smiling at Mrs. Garcia who sits with a canvas at the island, ever the early riser. For the last year, she's been working on her own prints to display in her gallery, and they've been flying off the walls.

"Hola, señora Garcia," I say, smiling her way.

I took Spanish for years, trying to understand the lyrics of Britt's bilingual works, to learn every melody whispered from her lips between kisses and conversations. But that wasn't the only reason. I used to picture us together for longer, forever before I stopped believing in it. Before I realized that love was something I wasn't sure how to truly do right. I used to imagine marrying her, back when we were little enough to play games like *house* and pretend to make a home. Before we did whatever we do now, before I ever kissed her. There was a time, I'd imagine falling into this family like it was my own, having a meal at a dinner table without ingesting sorrow between bites.

Britt's family has always welcomed me. Now, I don't know how much I'll see them either, once she goes.

Five days.

"Hola, Mia." She smiles back, and lets me see the picture, a nighttime carnival with a girl on the top of a Ferris wheel. Britt always makes her way into Mrs. Garcia's compositions, and I wish I had that, that my mom was here, that I could know if, when she sang, she ever thought of me.

She is here. I have the envelopes. I have this piece of her. I have five days. I just need to find the answers and I can have her, finally.

There's only one place for me to go next.

MIA

It's an unspoken rule in Sunset Cove that no one returns to Back to Me & You before the sun sets. Yet, I sit out on the curb like I used to, and the pink building behind me has lost some of its mystery at this hour, but none of its allure.

I reread the lyrics on the yellow envelope while I wait.

I'd build a shrine to keep you, even when you're gone,
I'd build a castle to show you, show you all my love,
I'd whisper sweet nothings to the dusk and dawn,
All to bring you back to our reckless love.
But instead I return to basics, to where it all began,
I trek the trail of memories, your hand not in my hand.
I start and I unravel and I find closure in our end,
But all I really want is that sweet beginning again.

Right now, Britt is practicing, laughing with the band. This week is the first time I've missed seeing Lost Girls rehearse in over three years. It's the first time I'm not sitting in the corner and penning new sheet music to accompany the lyrics. Instead, I stare out at the parking lot as a black sports car pulls in.

Britt said let's get a sign, so here I am.

The driver steps onto the pavement, shaking purple hair out of her face and flicking on her cat-eye sunglasses as she walks toward the building. Places as cool as this one always need time to put on their best illusions, and it looks like Edie's opening today.

I get to my feet, and when Edie sees me, her smirk flips on its axis. Still, she heads toward me, sparing me a distant once-over and moving to open the door, past a trash bin and empty bottles.

"Hi," I say to this woman of my mother's past.

"What do you want?" Her voice is cold but there's something else, just like there was in her stare the evening before. She kicks a can out of her way.

I cut right to it. "You knew my mom." I'm tired of giving in, I'm tired of wondering without the truth, piecing her together behind the scenes. She deserves more than this. And I need these stories. Now.

Edie's silence is an answer of its own.

She fumbles with her keys. "I can't talk to you about this."

"You were in her band. You were the lead guitarist," I say when she studies her reflection in the glass doors instead of me. I hold the envelope closer and step forward. "And now she's left me a hunt to find out more about her. I know you know about it. She wanted me to meet you." She's the first person besides Britt I've told about the hunt, and this pressure releases at the truth.

Edie turns, such sharp agony in the thin line of her lips. "I was wondering if that's why you were here."

"It's why I was here last night too."

Another spell of silence.

I continue because she won't. "Why did you come up to me in the first place? If you were only going to say I look like her and mess me up and leave?" The questions are quiet.

"I never said that outright." Her gaze drops.

"You recognized me as her daughter."

Now, she looks at me. "Kid, this whole town recognizes you as her daughter. That's what you are, who you are."

I flinch, falling back into my echoing. It's everything I want to be and everything I'm scared to become. "Why haven't I seen you before?"

"Because I made sure you didn't."

"Why?"

She leans against the pink wall, crossing her arms. She looks young—like she never quite grew into her age. There's something in her posture—a side-effect of the music—that tells me she's still that up-and-coming lead guitarist inside, no matter how many years are lost.

I lean against the wall too, trying to look as solemn and convincing as she does. What would Tori Rose do? My mom was in a band with Edie. She must have known how to talk to her. But I can't find the right words—I never can—so I hand her the lyrics instead. I take a leap, passing the yellow envelope to Edie with shaking hands.

Her brows furrow before she passes it right back to me without a second thought. "I can't help you."

"But you're part of this," I say. She moves for the door. "Please. I need to know her. I need to find this." Tears spark, and everyone I love has left or been left. Everyone I know has found something more.

Edie pauses in the doorframe, hand on the glass, key in the lock. She pulls it open, eyes on mine all the while. She looks like she's about to say something, as Grams and Nana so often do when they're on the brink of revealing her, but she closes the door, disappearing into Tori Rose's tribute club.

Nana's in my room. She sits crisscross on my comforter, waiting for me. Unlike Edie, proximity to the music aged her. She's still got freckles within the folds of her laugh lines and a mischievous look beneath—the same look Mom has in leftover pictures. But Nana's expression has softened and worn with pain, whereas Tori Rose's is forever free.

"Hey." I jostle my purse, letting the notebook sink deeper into it. "Is everything okay?" Is she going to ask? Does she want to know what her daughter left me?

She says, "How was your sleepover?"

"It was good."

"How's Britt?" Nana pats the bed beside her.

I toss my purse onto the chair, sitting next to her and pulling my legs under me. "Good. Happy. She's leaving soon." She already knows this from family dinners.

Gently, Nana's hand rises to my back, smoothing small circles over my spine. "I'm sorry, honey. I know how much she means to you."

The guilt is suffocating, sitting here with her, but I can't show my grandmas the hunt yet, not until they show that they want to know. I can't tell them how much it aches to see everyone else find something to dream about, find *themselves*. How much it hurts to see that my mother did too.

"Yeah, well, I have you guys." And I thank everything that's true. "It's fine. Really. I knew she'd leave."

Nana's hand stills, and panic washes over me. "How are you feeling about college?"

The shutters close around my heart. "It's college. More school." I recall their faces when I told them my post-high-school plan—community college, the inn—and how relieved they were.

She laughs softly, pressing a kiss to my forehead and smoothing a couple of stubborn hairs away from my cheeks. Her blouse is wrinkled, and I'm sure I'll find her ironing it and everything else in the house, like she does when she gets antsy, within the next couple weeks. "You're going to do great things, Mia Peters."

I am going to do nothing.

"Thanks, Nana."

Getting to her feet, she heads to the door. She stops there for a second, tosses me a glance. "We were thinking of doing lunch in twenty minutes. Our specialty."

"Ordering pizza?"

"You got it."

As soon as she's gone, I flop back onto my bed, folding my hands across my stomach and staring at the ceiling. At my side, a picture catches my eye.

It sits in a silver frame on my nightstand amidst Post-it notes scribbled with chords and lyrics Britt left. It's at graduation, with Britt—a snapshot my grandmas must have taken when we weren't looking, framed, and left for me. This was before Jess found me, before I broke up with him, as we were getting ready to walk that stage. Despite the panic that made its home within me that day, in this image, we're laughing with our caps tilted and hands intertwined.

We're laughing and I'm looking at her in a way I didn't even know I was capable of. It's the first time I see it. The image of my mom under the floorboard of her room, all soft-eyed and hopeful for the camera, returns to me. Here, I look like her. Really look like her in my own eyes, in a way that feels like it matters.

The journal, graduation, college, the curb outside Back to Me & You, last night at Britt's piano—all of them are held in this frame. Every push and pull, denial and acceptance, as I hug it to my chest.

And, of course, the first time I truly find my mother in myself comes when I'm with Britt. She's the personification of a love song, and I can't get her out of my head. Especially not now, not knowing the offer that remains. *You're the first person I want to cheer with.* In my mind's eye I know it all: her magic laugh, the feel of her lips, her skin under my fingertips, her voice, the stories she tells me late at night, the brilliant songs she writes, the furrow of her brows when she calls me out, the smirk on her lips when she's right yet again.

I lean further into the mattress, groaning because I can't figure *us* out right now either, and I set the picture down, picking the diary up once more.

With Britt still at rehearsal and the yellow envelope's lyrics speaking of rewinding time, I go to the very beginning of my mother's story, desperate to find something new to share.

It's well-known that Tori Rose was born in the attic of the inn before it was an inn. Before Peters' Inn became Roses & Thorns, back when the building was a tiny cinema run by my grandmas' good friend and they lived up here together—before they came back and bought the place.

I pull the ladder down from the ceiling, climb one rung at a time, leave that nursery behind, and emerge into the space.

> *I start and I unravel and I find closure in our end,*
> *But all I really want is that sweet beginning again.*

This was her beginning. This was her end. It's where she was born, where I assume my grandmas stored the gift before they gave it to me grad night, where she wrote her songs before that last tour—one of the accidental details I saved from overheard conversations.

Boxes are piled in every corner, and a lamp illuminates the space as best it can. Taking a deep breath, I open the yellow envelope, pushing aside everything except this. I read its contents, ready for more pages.

Mia,

I wondered if you'd find your way here. I hope you've had many good times in these walls too. Leaving this place behind without a proper goodbye is one of my biggest regrets.

As I write this, I'm looking out a tour bus window. And I have all this. I finally have it. I live for it. But I'm looking out this window, and I'm picturing the sea back home while I write my next song.

Hold on to your memories, love. They'll get you through the lonely days. Can you see the sea with me?

Love,
Mom

Hold on to your memories. I'm trying, Mom.

Placing the envelope out of the way, I get to work. I spend hours searching, setting aside old yearbooks and tour photos that I've encountered a few hundred times. I find the picture of her in senior year with the rest of her class, wearing a lacy dress before the inn's cherry blossoms. David Summers and his blond hair and sudden familiarity are just a couple of spaces over. But there's nothing else. I empty every yet-to-be-opened and already-open box. The pieces of her pile around me, but no matter where I look in the attic, there are those same cherry blossoms beyond the window and the pool in between. Nothing else. Nothing more.

I can't see the sea with her.

MIA

PRESENT DAY

"Mia, come here." Linnea calls from the corner, hunched over the karaoke machine with her pink toolbox.

After a restless night avoiding sleep while helping Britt shop at Sunset Cove's twenty-four-hour convenience store, I still haven't found my mother's beginning. If it's not the attic or any of the other rooms I searched at the inn, where does she consider it to be?

Leaving the saltshakers I'm refilling at the counter, I duck through the half-crowded room to where Linnea sits, repairing the machine my mother loved, *finally*. Its red exterior catches the overhead lights and the sun sliding through the open windows. The posters on the wall all stare at it—especially Tori Rose's.

I stare along with them. Two microphone chords intertwine and loop toward the steps leading to the Horizon's stage—the exact ones my mom sang through. Which did she use?

"How's it going?" I sit on the bottom step, a foot from where Linnea's polishing the machine.

She wipes her forehead with the sleeve of her flannel. Her white hair is held out of her way by a large clip. "Good, kiddo. I'm about ready for it to be tested." There's a meaning beneath her words, something suggestive.

"Oh."

"I invited Lost Girls over later. Thought you'd get a kick out of them rechristening it." Her grin is wider than I've seen it in a while.

"Oh, yeah of course." I pick at the rip in my jeans, exposing a small scar on my knee from the time Britt and I thought fencing was a good idea. It's not even from the sword—it's from tripping over a rock, distracted, looking at her.

"I just need help moving it back onto the stage. Not as agile as I used to be." Linnea gestures for me to lift from the other side, and I weave around, bending my knees and getting the best grasp I can on the sleek, boxy machine.

"One, two, three . . ."

We lift, and somehow I end up moving backward up the steps, one step at a time. The karaoke machine trembles in our shared grip, heavy as a memory. I reach behind me for the top step, searching with my right foot as Linnea says, "Just a sec . . ."

It's not clear who moves at the wrong time or if we both do, but the machine tumbles out of our hands, hitting the hardwood floor with a noise that's anything but musical.

"Oh, shit. Shit. Shit. Shit." I hurry off the stage, crouching beside it. How do I always manage to mess things up when it comes to Tori Rose? Maybe *this* is a sign.

"Oh, hey, hey, kid, it's okay." Linnea rushes over to me, tipping it upright again. "Nothing broke. This thing is solid." She knocks on the side of it. "It's outlasted worse, trust me."

"I'm so sorry, Linnea."

"Hon, I slipped. What are you sorry for?" She's watching me so closely, I have to look away, scrubbing at my cheek. "Come on. Help me get it up. Let's try this one more time."

Her expression doesn't leave room for argument, so I do as she says, steadying myself against the stage. But just as I glance at where my hand rests against the planks, I note the subtle carvings next to my thumb, hidden on the edge, almost fully disguised by dust and splinters, something new that I've never seen.

TR was here.

The karaoke machine is christened with "Don't Stop Believin'" in Lost Girls's haunting voices. Standing behind the counter, chin in my palm, I watch Britt walk from one side of the stage to the next in her blue jeans and favorite T-shirt—a Taylor Swift concert shirt. Linnea managed to find a third mic somewhere in storage, and Sophie uses it now, arm slung over Amy's shoulders.

But even as they perform, Britt's eyes never leave mine, and that's how I know she picked this song for me.

The second it's over, notes fading into afternoon chatter, she hops down first, making her way to where I stand next to Linnea who's wiping away tears. The customers cheer, and two boys in boardshorts—hair still damp from the ocean and wakeboards leaning against their chairs—take the mics next. Sophie and Amy grab a table.

"What did you find?" Britt holds up her phone and the keyboard slam text I'd sent her along with a picture that apparently won't download.

Linnea looks back and forth between us, so I wrap around

the counter, taking the stool next to Britt and spinning closer to her. "You're going to be a star, you know that, right?"

She shakes her head. "Stars burn out. I want to be my own goddamn galaxy."

Those words linger, and my gaze falls to her lips before I force it back to her brown eyes.

"Of course," I say, and she smiles.

"What did you find?" Britt repeats, sitting too as Linnea walks over to Sophie and Amy.

"Initials," I say. "On the edge of the stage. Like in the light-house."

"So you think she began here," Britt finishes.

"Well, her adventure kind of did. But I looked around on my shift. There's nothing behind the frames, nothing beneath any of the planks, and I'm pretty sure Linnea thinks I'm hiding some-thing, which at this point, aren't I?" It all comes out in a rush.

Britt shrugs. "Or you're finding something."

"Or that," I whisper.

She taps the beat of the song she just finished against the countertop. "Did you check the attic?"

"At the inn? Yeah. It's the first place I looked."

"No. The attic here." She waves in the general direction of above us and twists the charm bracelet around her wrist. There's a new charm, a fourth one—a little suitcase.

I reach out, tracing over the intricate designs. "What's this one?"

She blushes. "It's from Dania and Mile last night. They said not just any suitcase can hold all my dreams."

My heart pinches at the notion. "I love that . . . There's an attic here?" How have I worked here for three years and never known that?

Her eyes brighten with the secret, and she waves for me to follow her. "Linnea?" Britt walks over to her.

Linnea looks up from where she sits, grinning and talking with Sophie and Amy. "What's up? Great song, by the way, hon."

"Thanks." I swear Britt glows. "I need to research for another song. This might be my last chance here. Can Mia and I go to the attic?"

Last chance.

"Of course." Linnea turns back to the two other girls.

With that, Britt beckons for me to follow again, and once more, I do. We wind behind a violet door into the small kitchen with its metal surfaces and plentiful windows. The waves rush on the beach just ahead of this place, caressing the sand.

Can you see the sea with me?

She's onto something.

Hopping onto the stool by the counter, Britt pulls the beaded string hanging down from the ceiling. The ladder slides to the ground before us, eerily reminiscent of the entrance to the attic from the nursery.

"I've never been up here before." My voice echoes as we climb.

Reaching the top, taking it in with her hands on her hips, Britt says, "Well then it's your turn."

"For what?" I join her.

She doesn't answer—she doesn't need to—because I step up into the Horizon's attic and I see for myself. It's like every person in this town decided to store something here. It's all the forgotten and misused pieces of Sunset Cove collected in one room. There are abandoned instruments, dust-covered paintings, and bent records all forming a graveyard of the arts. The large back window creates an odd, tenuous glow. When I move toward that glass, I note it's not stained like the pattern suggests. It's covered by a layer of old, scratched-up paint.

"I can't see the sea anymore." My fingertips trace along the hues of pink and orange.

"You can a little bit." Britt comes up beside me. "If you really look between those markings in the paint."

"What are they?" They spread out around us, causing a sort of lit-up pattern to form across the floor.

She takes a step back, and moves toward the boxes, trailing her nails across the dust. "I don't know. It's not what I was looking for the first time."

"How did you know so much was up here?"

She glances my way, and her smirk is wicked. "Where do you think I got the stories for the song I performed at the festival? The night we . . ."

First kissed. Slipup number one.

That evening still whispers across my skin when I envision it no matter how many years pass. It was the summer before freshman year, and we'd been something between friends and crushes for weeks, but that was the day we really blurred the lines.

It was after her music drew me in all over again—after she wove Sunset Cove's tales into melodies at the summer festival. We snuck away to the quiet cove we'd discovered that May, far from the squealing, cotton candy breezes, whirring rides, flashing lights. With our toes dipped in the sea, our fingers slightly crinkled from the ocean waves, the salt of it in her brown hair, I'd told her, "That was magic." Because it was, because she was.

I still don't know who kissed who first.

Neither of us fills the silence, and she lets the memories of what she built on that festival's stage trail off. For someone so set on getting out of here, she sure knows how to make her mark.

After a long moment, I say, "Well, I guess it's just a matter of looking for what she wanted us to find."

Britt doesn't reply, but we search together. In this place marked by my mom's beginning, my hunt for another of Tori Rose's truths starts. I tie my hair up in a scrunchie, clear surfaces, and search through the lost history of Sunset Cove. I imagine her trying to climb through this hurricane-aftermath of a space just to leave a clue for me.

Time passes in silence, and time passes in whispered *Look at this*'s and *Come here*'s. It isn't awkward—not with Britt—but it's heavy knowing I won't even have the silence with her, let alone the music, in such a short time.

All I can think of is Lost Girls and "Don't Stop Believin'" and that night at the piano. I've seen what the music can do. I've seen how it works. My mother was so brave, so wild-hearted. The music took her away, left my grandmas to cope with no goodbye and unspoken grief.

Focus.

Those strange spots of sunlight from the painted window blur in front of me. I blink them away until they seem like a message too. Even that illumination seems to mock us, to signal yet another place in this town where she rests, and then I realize *it does*.

It's letters—not scratches. It's a message—not a warning.

"We need to clear the floor," I say.

"Why?" Britt's got a feather boa looped around her neck and a cowgirl hat pulled low over her head that she tips my way.

This time, my smile's true, full. The weight lifts, if only momentarily. "Because that's where the story is."

I flit from box to box, sliding them aside. There's a fifty-fifty chance Linnea will ban us for rearranging her mess. She likes to organize, to do everything herself. But that won't matter. This attic, in each of our visits, has given us both what we needed. If I'm ever allowed back in it after today, though, I'll ask Linnea why she's kept these things, why she's built her own shrine up here to this town that made us all.

It takes another half hour of stacking, carefully arranging the space into something like the lovechild of Tetris and Jenga before the space is clear. Grabbing a broom that was leaning against the corner, I sweep away dust bunnies and unearth the hardwood. My mother's words are cross-stitched in light. They slip through the painted gaps on the window's surface and spell out lyrics from the envelope across the floor:

I start and I unravel and I find closure in our end,
But all I really want is that sweet beginning again.

A heart carved out of more sunlight sits next to the lit-up words, right over a loose floorboard where *TR was here* has been written again.

I lock eyes with Britt and pry the plank up with my fingers. Beneath, nestled in the cleared-out space, is the next chapter of her story.

TORI

1989

Sara Ellis left me a note to meet her at Centennial Park.

The sun touched the sky, and I was out the door. I slipped down the hall, leaving David sleeping (snoring with his mouth open and drooling slightly onto his pillow) in bed. There was no sign of life from outside Patrick Rose's room, so I slipped across the hall and knocked. I pressed my ear to the door when he didn't answer. Nothing.

No one else was in the hallway at this time. I clasped my hands behind my back. The music waited for me outside. At the park. He'd have to meet me there.

I left the hotel and the man behind the counter (in a fox-printed vest this morning). Ducking through streets that danced with melodies, I crossed a city where I felt like Tori Rose *belonged.*

The whole way there, I studied everything I could. The signs. The brick. The people.

The second I made it to Centennial Park, I asked for

directions to the Parthenon. The grass was green, and the sky was bright with the sun that caressed my shoulders.

Sara laid with her keyboard on her chest, looking at the clouds as she played a chromatic scale in C major. In jeans and a purple T-shirt, she looked ready for this. For the music. Next to her, Mateo and Edie played rock paper scissors.

Edie's hair was in pigtails and a grin stretched across her purple-painted lips as she beat Mateo again.

He was in a denim jacket, brown eyes shining and angled toward Sara slightly. There was something there.

"Hi," I said to them all.

Sara turned her head toward me, and she rolled her eyes at the others, but she didn't get up. "Hey, sit down. We're going to write a hit."

"Yeah, sit down." Edie echoed, and Sara shoved her lightly.

I did. I was never one for taking directions, but I listened to this girl promising the music to me. The last few nights, the band had sat in a writers round in the empty event room of the hotel and tried to come up with our own song. We had an open mic we'd managed to secure a spot at, coming up. But nothing sounded right. Patrick had been oddly silent through it all, slipping out early the last two nights.

Still no sign of him.

He'd be here soon.

As long as we had the music, we were doing what we were supposed to.

The other night, I'd asked Sara how she found her songs. I knew where I got my lyrics in Sunset Cove, but Sunset Cove wasn't good enough for Music City. Now, she started us off. I loved that she lugged a keyboard to a quiet park. I loved that she thought to bring the music with her where she went. Linnea's words from the Horizon came back to me. I wasn't the only one anymore.

The music built. Sara didn't sing. She truly was a master-class pianist. The way the chords she played told a story was unlike anything I'd heard.

Her eyes opened for a second and her brows raised my way. In a dare.

I took it.

I found lyrics to go with her tune, and the notes she played swelled to meet them.

> *So I tell you to light the world on fire,*
> *For this was a lesson I quickly learned.*
> *I'll sit here on my side of the world, you on yours,*
> *And together we'll watch it burn.*
> *There was a melody in your fire, a reckoning in your truth.*
> *Honey, I think that all the songs I sing were meant to*
>   *capture you,*
> *And on this starlit night, with the flame and with the sea,*
> *You start a fire in your heart, and you make it burn for me.*

Mateo pulled out his drumsticks. Made the beat against the grass. Edie joined him. She played her guitar.

Lyrics wound around us, tangling in our hair and hearts. When the song ran out, my gaze locked with Sara's. Edie's. Mateo's.

Sara shook her head. "Still not right."

I nodded.

We began again.

By the time the sun sank down in the sky, Edie got bored and Mateo had a shift at a nearby record store where he worked.

Sara asked if I'd stay behind. And I said yes. I knew neither of us was leaving until we'd done what we came for.

"Why'd you join Fate's Travelers?" I asked.

"You ask a lot of questions, Tori Rose."

"I know."

She sat up and pulled one knee to her chest, propping her elbow on it. "I like the rush of performing with someone's eyes to meet across the stage. Mateo and I had already planned to work together, and I liked Edie's energy. Something fit that night, and when I have a gut feeling, I'm not really one to question it. One day, I want to do this on my own, but right now I want to share the music. That's what this is all about, no?" She shook her head. "I want to be part of something big. I want to *make* something big. I think Fate's Travelers could be something if we try. I knew I could turn it into something great. I think you see it too."

I scooted closer to her, and our shoulders brushed. She smiled and it was a wicked expression that made my stomach flutter. "I do."

Sara stretched. "Why'd you join?"

"I needed people who would carry a keyboard to a park for no reason. Who would sing at nothing. Everything. I needed to not be the only one with a song to share. The second I walked into that party, I felt like the music came alive in meeting all of you."

"That blond boy who walks you to practice, is he a musician?"

"No, my best friend."

"I see." The chords we'd strung together dissipated for a minute. Something else formed. "How did you meet Patrick?" She began to play some notes again in a way that seemed like she didn't even realize she was doing it. In a way that made music a habit.

She asked about Patrick, who never showed up.

I sighed. "He came to my town, sang at prom, and I joined him. I couldn't help it. There was something in his voice. He made the story his own. How'd you meet Mateo?"

"I used to busk on Music Row. This one boy always came. He left me notes in my keyboard case, and it went from there. I guess some songs lead us to who we're destined to find. Some are a beginning, and some are an end."

Her last words pause the moment and my train of thought at once. "That's *it*. You're brilliant."

"I know, but why?" She studied me.

I reached for one of the many loose papers around us. She began to play as I scrawled across the page. I whisper-sang and she changed the tempo. She tweaked the beat in such a perfect way (a little bit of pop mixed into country). A dancing song. A performance song.

She nodded along. "This is it."

Around 2 a.m., the sky opened. Sara and I packed up in a rush, racing under weeping leaves and trees with our coats shielding our hair. She ran off, barely saying goodbye, but the song we'd written said it for us. I watched her slip down the street, through blinking headlights.

"Hey, you cold?" A voice came from behind me, and I spun around. David stood with a black umbrella sporting Dolly Parton's enlarged face across it. His yellow raincoat matched the cheer of his grin.

"What are you doing?" I'd left him a note saying where I went so he wouldn't worry (or call my moms), but I didn't expect him to join me.

He shrugged. "Thought you might need someone to remind

you to look up from whatever you were working on. You left a long time ago. You know it's tomorrow, right?"

"Technically, it's today."

He shook his head, extending the umbrella. I stepped under it with him.

"Where's Rose Boy?" he asked, and I linked my arm through his, stealing his warmth as we speed-walked.

"I . . ." He never came.

David's gaze was steady on my face in the way that tried to pry for everything. He didn't even mean to.

I took the umbrella from him, and I closed it. The rain pounded down on us, and I laughed, staring up at the crying sky. The tune Sara and I had just written flowed through me as David smiled.

"Dance with me," I said. "It's the perfect weather."

He shook his head, took a bow, and extended a hand. I looped my arms around his neck. I let the song Sara and I wrote spin through my head and tried not to wonder too hard why the boy with the rose tattoo couldn't be bothered to show up for a song, locking my blue eyes on David's green ones.

His loose waves plastered his tanned forehead. "So . . . you write a hit?"

Spinning away from him, I opened the umbrella again. "What do you think?"

I knocked on Patrick Rose's door when David returned to our room. After three times, he finally opened it. He wore disappointingly plain pajama pants that made me think of the many themed pairs David owned, and he leaned against the door jam.

His gaze was sheepish, and that was all the proof I needed. He'd chosen to miss today.

I shook my head and met his blue eyes with mine. "I don't know you."

He laughed. "You're just realizing this?" His eyes held that same carefree nature. But the excitement of a strange boy in a familiar town had faded. Everything was new here, and I needed him to be with me in this.

"You show up at my prom. You promise the music. And then you don't show? What were you doing today?"

"I . . . do you want to go for a walk?"

"I want to know why you broke your promise."

His brows furrowed. "My *promise?*"

"You said you were here for the music. You said we were following it together."

"Tori . . ."

"Yes?"

I waited, a breath passed, then another. A million possibilities filled the quiet. He could've not known what to say. Been replaying our practices in his head. Thinking. Wondering.

"I . . ." He shook his head.

I was prepared for any of those possibilities, but I wasn't prepared for the boy with the rose tattoo to shut the door.

"WHAT IF WE"

From Tori Rose's 1994 album That Summer

MIA

"You girls were up there a while," Linnea says when Britt and I return downstairs.

What was left of the crowd has mostly cleared, but a few still linger at tables. They have snacks and drinks under the thrum of my mother's songs playing on loop from Sunset Cove's only station. They sit in beach clothes and bathing suits and ripped jeans. They don't realize what just took place above their heads.

"Thanks for letting us look," I say, standing in this room at the same time I'm sitting in Centennial Park with Sara Ellis and Tori Rose as they wrote Fate's Travelers' first hit. I'm soaking in the rain as she danced with David. I'm watching Patrick Rose shut the door while, here, I watched Britt's gaze spark when Sara and my mother wove lyrics and music together. There are more questions, there are more answers, and Tori Rose was so sure.

Each page makes it clearer she was meant to leave, clearer she couldn't find what she needed here. This town gives and takes so much, but the way she paints the spotlight and the dream? It glows.

"Sure thing," Linnea says and smiles, bringing me back to the present. She erases a couple numbers on her sudoku, and a confession is on the tip of my tongue. I don't know why, but I want to tell her what we found over her diner, to see if someone else shares this threatening pulse between their rib cage at my mother's courage.

I haven't even told my grandmas, and Edie couldn't have cared less, but Linnea is open and sitting there, and I know she'll keep my secrets and my mother's too. A part of me needs someone besides me and Britt in this town to believe that Tori Rose was not just her time in the limelight, but she was also more than her forced fall from grace.

Mom must have trusted her, to have spent all that time in the attic painting that window. Linnea resurrected the karaoke machine. She got that little piece of her back. As I replay what Sara said to my mother, *I want to share the music. That's what this is all about, no?*, the first words come out in a whisper.

"Linnea, do you want to know what we were looking for?" The secrets fill me to the brim, and they cut me open on their way to my lips.

"More songs, right?"

"No. Not quite."

Britt's eyes widen, and she pokes my hip.

I turn to her, nod. *I'm ready*, I hope that says.

"All right, hit me." Linnea leans forward across the counter, and I think she's ready too.

I begin with grad night, with the gift, and I let Linnea in on the hunt, on these days of chasing the reasons for my mother's dreams and wondering why I'm not more like her in that way, wanting my own to follow—but I leave that last part out.

"She . . ." When I finish, Linnea's eyes are even mistier than during "Don't Stop Believin'"—not their usual bright amber.

"She had that up there all along? That's . . . oh, God, when she asked to go to the attic, I thought she was looking for something. I didn't realize she was saying goodbye." Tears slip down her cheeks, and my chest tightens.

Wrapping her arms around my shoulders, even with the counter between us, Linnea pulls me close, like she would when I was little and hung out here after school as my grandmas finished up work and met me for dinner. She pulls me close like she did both me and Britt the night of our last song in public together, swaying me from side to side.

"Maybe I shouldn't have . . ." I start as a sob shakes her body.

"No." She pulls back, gripping my arms so I meet her eyes, which are blazing. "Thank you for sharing this with me."

Britt's halfway through a blueberry muffin behind us, sitting at the counter and folding the wrapper. Her eyes shout something to me that I can't decipher, endless ambition in her irises, everything she wants to prove, and mine hide my wonderings about the neon lights of Music City and an adventure with this girl. If I didn't have the story to face, if I was just me and she was just her and we were just us, I wonder what it would be like to sit beneath the leaves of Centennial Park together.

The seat beside Britt is empty, and I slip into it, leveling my gaze with Linnea, who's still wiping at her eyes and catching glances.

"So how many clues are left?" she asks.

"Four." This will be the first real goodbye I'll have to say to my mom, the first time I lose my own memories of her. We're halfway through the entries. I'm not ready for that farewell, not ready for her absence to hit harder than it ever has, so I know that the next clues must be everything. But I also know I need them fast, in these next few days. I need my answer.

Britt squeezes my knee, under the counter, and I exhale.

"What did she say in the diary?" Linnea asks.

I continue, "She told me about her journey, about why she left this town and where she went. She's still telling me how she got there, what she's doing, and about her rise to fame." I glance at where the old karaoke machine sits on the stage, where it should be. "She mentioned that machine."

Linnea sniffs, wipes her eyes on the hem of her apron. "I just couldn't listen to it anymore after her. I didn't let anyone perform on that stage for years after she passed, because it was hers. She was a hurricane, that girl. And when you asked about her the other day, about how she . . . I wanted to give you a piece of her music and life. I should've done it sooner. But it was too hard."

"I get that," I whisper. "It's impossible to forget her here." I glance at Britt, hoping to convey a little bit about why I'm here, why I still need to stay. "There are memories living in this town from Back to Me & You to record stores that say *Hey, she was here.* But it's hard too, because she's *everywhere.* I've never known how to really know her for everything she was. I've never known how to leave the little pieces of her I have or the people who need to hold on to those stories without saying them."

"The magic of small towns," Britt says, and there's the slightest bitterness to it.

"Truly." The pause is too much. "How close were you two?" I glance back at Linnea, because I've never asked, and she never told me, but she clearly knows more than she lets on.

Linnea sighs. "Your mother was born here, lived in the town for twelve years, and then left for a while with her moms. When they got on their feet and were ready, they came back and bought the inn. The first time she was here, that girl would come and raise chaos. I was in junior high at the time and working with my pops. I used to be her babysitter. She'd weave in and out of my space, singing wherever she went. She had this ridiculous pink harmonica she wouldn't part with. She slept with it like a security blanket, and then she got her first guitar and she would come and ask to play me all her songs." She's getting teary again.

Britt hands her a napkin—this torn-up look on her face that destroys me. Neither of us has seen Linnea Rodgers cry before.

Linnea waves this off, holding tight to Britt's hand. "I'm okay. I just try not to relive it too often. It was when we were older, after her first few tours and her band split up and she came back for a visit, that we got really close. She missed her moms, but she was dead set on getting back to the road. She never did find herself comfortable here. Never wanted to stay. We talked a lot back then. She told me about life in Music City and how she'd found her place. I told her . . ." Linnea trails off, and I'm about to reach out, to tell her despite how I want to know, she doesn't have to finish if it's hard, if it hurts too much. "She was the only one I told about the life I wanted. With a family. Kids, before I found out I couldn't have any. Adoption process was hell with all the getting my hopes up and getting crushed. She asked what I'd name my kid if I had one, and we dreamed together."

She never did find herself comfortable here. Never wanted to stay. Is that my answer? But how can it be? Why would she show me around the magic of this town, show me the pain in her wake, if she didn't want it to keep me?

Britt's fingers drum against the counter, always the one to keep her head, to push forward, to search for what people refused to say. "What would you name your kid?"

Linnea's expression is the kind someone gets when they're recalling the best of times before the worst of times. In this moment, here at the counter of the Horizon where I've been frequenting my entire life, she says one word and it shatters my world: "Mia."

MIA

When I walk Britt home, she pauses on the front porch step, glances back over her shoulder, and waves. My heart twists and twists, but I wave too before she opens the door, and walks inside. As soon as she's gone, I run.

My purse and the journal within it swing at my side. It's too far to race, but too close not to, so I weave my way through the Technicolor streets as fairy lights wink along porch rails. Tori Rose's voice wraps around every bit of Sunset Cove from outdoor speakers that project the radio. Her lyrics are graffitied along buildings.

When I reach the inn, I grab my bike, holding the rose charm tight before I sling one leg over the seat and pedal off. The revelation gives me wings, and I use them to fly down the quiet road, to the one place I know I need to go.

My mother did more than give this town its fame. She began and ended in so many places: at the inn, at the Horizon, at the lighthouse, on the radio, by the sea. She's touched every inch of this place. Tori Rose is everywhere from the breeze to the monuments in her honor, but it turns out she's also reached the hearts here. She also cared enough to make real connections, like David Summers, like *Linnea*. She left and still loved it, she moved on but not completely.

She did both.

She named me for Linnea, for a person she met here. She led me to Linnea's diner to unearth this. She wanted me to find it. She wanted me to know that in her life, she crossed states and seas, and all the while, Sunset Cove meant something to her too.

Edie's here early again, behind the bar. I knock, loud and clear on the glass door. I need her answers. I need her side of this story. I will wait from dusk to dawn if that's what it takes for her to tell me, for her to help me find my mother. I've got four days going on three, and I saw the way Lost Girls *lived* on that stage today, became the song.

Now, more than ever, knowing my mom needed to leave but held this town in her heart, I have to know what she had to say. What would she tell me to do about my summer? Is it possible for me to have the road and keep Sunset Cove, to not lose everything to it?

The sun beats down, the ocean breeze barely carries here, and the lights of the city beyond aren't far. I stay still, waiting. It's hours until the doors will burst open beneath the first traces of sunset. But I can wait.

Edie's eyes flit up from where she's polishing the shot glasses lining the dark marble counter, and her brows furrow. Taking her time, she wipes her hands on her stained white apron, and makes her way around the bar. She walks across the tile, her steel-toed boots drag, until there's nothing left to delay. She stands on one side of the glass, and I'm on the other as she unlocks the door.

"I thought I told you I couldn't help," she whispers, but there's not the assertion behind it hours later, just the pain. Her face is clean of makeup, and it softens her.

"You have to." I clasp my hands behind my back to stop them from shaking. "No one will tell me about her. Or if they will, they don't know enough. They don't know *her*. I don't know why you're part of her hunt when you so clearly don't like me and don't want me near you but she—"

"You think that's what this is?" Edie's jaw loosens, her own clenched hands unravel. She leans against the door. "You actually think that?"

"I . . ." I shrug. What else is there to think?

Edie's heart is shattering across her features. All my time growing up around grief, and I didn't know a heart could break that openly.

"The clue you handed me yesterday, it's not one of the ones I'm supposed to help you with." Edie's voice, a new gentleness to it, holds my attention.

She mentioned a clue.

Between my heart's stumbling beats, I hesitate, not wanting to push her back into her shell. "You know multiple clues? You're supposed to help with more than one?"

"Two. What happened to the *Meet Me in the Lyrics* one?" She tugs a hand through her purple bangs and checks from one side of the parking lot to the other. We've still got time.

I pull the orange envelope out of my purse, and her gaze lands back on me. "I solved it."

"How?"

I shrug again because I can play this questions-and-no-answers game too. Edie looks at me deeper, differently than she did before. Today, she's not trying to place where she knows me like she did in the club. She's seeing how she doesn't.

Letting the door close behind her and joining me on the sidewalk, she walks away, around the side of the building.

"Where are you going?" *Not again.*

Walking backward, she wears the first genuine grin I've seen from her. It stops me in my tracks. "You coming?"

I'm coming.

Wrapping around the side of the club, Edie leads me to the fifth door, the room I found my mother's memorabilia in. She turns her own key in the lock.

"You have a key?" The beer case I used to keep the door open is crumpled but there, kicked to the side.

"Your mom made two keys," she says, propping the door open with another empty box as her walls fall. She takes in the empty spot in the frame where the pages used to be, nods, and sits crisscross on the floor, continuing, "One for me and . . . one she left for someone else to find. I take it you found it instead?"

The key sitting around my neck burns, and I nod. Who was it meant for? That house by the ocean breeze and rocks and sea—where Britt and I found it hidden under the mat— was empty. Completely. Who did she leave that collage on the wall, those "Remember Me" lyrics for? The same person? Did they see them, answer her? Did she find her way back to them?

"I'm sorry I didn't help you. That night or morning," Edie says as I sit across from her and lean against a box of old swag Britt and I already went through.

"Why didn't you?"

Edie does something I never expected. She tears up, and I'm terrible, empty, aching. Watching her, I know I'm the one who will never know how to grieve my mother properly, like those who can remember her. Every memory I've got is stolen, taken, or given by another.

"Your mom . . . Mia," it's like she's testing my name, seeing if she likes it, "she was my best friend. She was my sister and bandmate and she was so fucking alive. She was so determined to be a star that the world fell in love with her ambition. We all did. She set everyone she met ablaze. I met her and we bonded. When our band fell apart, we lost each other for a while and then found each other again. We grew from that."

I can't help wondering what happened between Fate's Travelers that left them with so much talent and only one album, if it had to do with Patrick Rose running away in that last section, if I'll find that in these pages too, but I hold my tongue. Edie's a fearful, reluctant storyteller, and I don't want to scare her off.

She keeps going. "She hated me after everything that happened and then she didn't, I envied her and then I didn't. Because the world raises girls to be competitors, not constellations. But we found our way to that place again. She became such a part of me. We would spend every holiday together. Playing with her was magic. It was madness. So when we found out"—Edie's voice cracks and my heart writhes—"when I found out we were going to have to say goodbye, I couldn't do it. She told me about the hunt, told me to help you, but seeing you, looking like her, I couldn't say goodbye again. I didn't think I could help you find her last words."

Found out . . . The first tears fall. Edie saw her in me too. Too much, not enough, forever a memory of Tori Rose, but then again, she also saw something different in me today. Something that has her really looking now, talking to me all the same.

"Thank you," I say rather than any of the other things bubbling up inside me.

Edie wipes at her own eyes with the backs of her hands. "No need to thank me."

"No, there is." I pause. "Because that's the most anyone has ever told me." Besides Linnea, besides my mom.

Edie sniffs, taking in the room around us and my mother's poster in the daylight. "Where are you heading for the next clue?"

"I just found the one in the Horizon."

"With Linnea?" Edie asks and I almost grin. Edie Davis of Fate's Travelers is here in a storage room with me, talking about the woman whose diner I grew up in.

"Yeah, with Linnea."

"Your mother did always love your name and that woman. She thought she was special. She thought you were special."

Scooting closer, I wait for more, hoping there is more, as vain as that seems. My mother thought I was special? Did she believe in me, in the dreams I would one day have? What would she *say*?

Before I can pry further, Edie says, "Are you ready for the next pages?"

MIA

When Edie leads me into the woods beyond Back to Me & You's parking lot, it seems like a good place to leave a body. I consider texting my grandmas, letting them know where I am as we disappear beneath a canopy of leaves, but they still think I'm with Britt and that's easier than explaining this, so I put my faith in my mother, and I shove my phone away.

The green envelope sits ready in my hands.

> *Bookended by legends and music, eyes met and we*
> *   slowly became,*
> *My heart was yours, yours was mine in every small way.*
> *Late at night I hear your laugh in the records we played,*
> *Haunted, I had you back then and will never know you*
> *   the same.*
> *I left it all for this road, for the promise it held,*
> *Left it all, left you too, left the love that we had,*
> *And I stare out the window, ask memories to take me home,*
> *But that house by the sea is no longer my own.*

The house by the sea. Will this reveal who owned it and who the key was meant for, who was supposed to find that storage room before me?

"We're almost there," Edie says.

I'm not turning around this far in. Earlier dances through my mind. I focus on the feeling of searching the attic of the Horizon with Britt and finding the way my mother and Sara Ellis wrote their hit, the way they made their stories start all on their own.

This feels like another start. Edie leads me into another world, a universe escaping the reaches of Sunset Cove and falling entirely into the legend of Tori Rose. When we stop, it sits before us.

Moss crawls up the sides and rust has eaten the bumpers. The windshield is clouded, and the golden rose painted across the side is faded with time. The windows are closed to the forest, and I step toward it.

My mother's tour bus. From *Forest in the Sea* to her very last album, *Regret You*. This is the vehicle that took her away.

"How the . . ." I shake my head.

Edie's about to place a hand on my shoulder before she thinks better of it. "Welcome to her second home."

"How did you . . ."

Taking it in with me, she gives a modest shrug. "I helped with this clue. She loved this thing. She lived in it more than she didn't. I was sure they were going to turn it into another roadside attraction, another way to make money off her, so we planned to keep it for ourselves, for you. When she—" Edie swallows sharply, her expression a constant seesaw between remembrance and forced forgetting. "I was with her on the last tour. When she . . . when she didn't come back with me, I drove this thing here myself. I was so fucking angry. I wanted to burn it and everything that outlived her. I took the back routes. I'd be swarmed otherwise. Gold diggers in this place, I swear. Couldn't stop trying to build off her light. I ran it through the trees. There's a road leading in here. It turns to gravel. Then dirt. Then nothing. It got stuck. I got stuck along with it here. Couldn't leave once I came."

She was with her on the last tour.

If it weren't so sad, if she wasn't so shattered, sticking a country star's tour bus in the middle of these small-town woods to grow into the forest might be funny. But it's not.

"Edie . . ."

She stiffens at her name. "It worked. No one saw it. I told them all it was lost with her guitar." Her story ends, her side of it closes.

"Edie, how did my mom die?" I think I know, but I just want someone to say it. I just want to know *for sure*. Was it the road or the fame or . . .

This makes her look at me. Her hand rises, and this time she does place it on my shoulder. "Oh, honey, she was sick. She fought so hard. To the bitter end, she tried."

The weight forever within me doubles at the same time that it shifts at the same time that it crashes down to crush my heart and my chest and . . . She told me. I know how my mother died. It wasn't the music. It was illness. She was stolen by life, not by a song. She would've been taken from us regardless of that last tour, regardless of whether she came home.

"I . . ." Sobs claw into my lungs and my throat, but I swallow them down, swallow down every question except what I want to know most. "Why did she go on that last tour?"

"To retire," Edie whispers. "To say goodbye. She thought she had more time."

The words float between us, and they're everything. *She wanted to come home.*

Edie clears her throat. "Do you want to see inside? I check on it. Now and then." Tears are slipping down her cheeks, and I nod. I let her breathe.

I'm ready for her to lead the way, to follow her inside. But she gestures for me to go, and she waits. I lead. I trace my way between the grass, pull open the bent door, and head up the silver steps.

While the outside is the forest's re-creation, the inside of this bus is entirely Tori Rose. Her heart, her soul, her passion are clear across the walls in signed records and framed photos of concerts and singers she admired. There's a small kitchen stuffed against one wall and a long pink couch along the back. Another step leads up to the leather driver and passenger seats, and a treble clef charm hangs from the dash. Sheet music is stuck to the walls from the end of her career to the beginning. Those notes lead down the hall, to the washroom, to the bedroom.

"You can go look," Edie says at my back, and I jump at the threshold of my mother's room.

The bed sits unmade, permanently rumpled, and there's a trail of sequined dresses and high heels along the floor. The photographs closest to her bed, framed on her bedside table are sparser. There's only three. One of her with her head on a blond boy's shoulder in front of the Horizon—David Summers. One of her with her arms around a dark-haired boy's neck beneath the looming presence of Nashville's Parthenon—Patrick Rose. And one of her sitting on that couch out there with a baby on her lap—me.

She looks so happy in every one, in every life.

I take the one of us and hold it close, examining the way she was caught in motion. Laughing. She was laughing, even with everything.

"You can take that with you." Edie whispers. "If you want. She'd want you to have it."

Slowly, I slip it into my purse, still examining the other two. "Thank you."

"It's not the only thing she'd want you to have."

I glance at where Edie's swaying toward the door, like she's about to be spooked again. But she stays, and I wait. With a quick wave of her hand, she beckons me, gestures for me to come.

She's climbing onto that couch before I can say anything, and I step forward, there if she falls.

"What are you doing? Do you want me to do that?"

Shaking her head, Edie pulls at the panels over the stairs leading to the wheel and those front seats. They slide away to reveal cobwebs and dust behind them, but also something pink. The curve of wood stained with roses.

I can't breathe as Edie pulls out my mother's original guitar. The sobs make their way out, but they're mixed with laughs too. Her careful gaze meets mine. She holds out the pink, painted instrument with a dent in the body and a broken string along the neck and frets.

There's a rose gold pick stuck in the strings.

I cradle it close, and it's the nearest I've ever felt to her. I can imagine her sitting behind me, guiding my fingers to the right places, teaching me how to play instead of the hours I spent learning online.

"It's *here*," the words escape between tears.

Nodding, Edie moves to the floor again. "It's yours. She wanted you to have it."

I sit too, pulling it into my lap despite the way the instrument jostles and creaks. Strumming a couple chords, I hum as Edie watches with wide-eyed fascination as if she hasn't seen a girl with a guitar before. My voice keeps quiet, stays low in her presence, but for a second, it wants out. I want to let it out.

"I painted those roses," Edie says, barely a murmur.

All those legends, all those myths, and Edie painted them.

I could ask her more right now. I could ask about my dad, see if I can finally find who he is. Edie would *know*. But just in this moment, I have more of my mom, the most I've ever had, more of her that's just mine, and this feels like it could be a direction, a sign, the start of the answer. She gave me her guitar. And I don't want to overshadow it, to cloud the meaning of what she left me. I want to honor her.

"What was her favorite song to play?" I ask, and Edie, once more, sits across from me.

"She loved 'Forest in the Sea.' Never told me why."

So I take a deep breath and I play and hum, almost ready to sing but not quite yet, not right here in front of her yet. I'm almost there, on my way, but I just need this moment to be what it is. The chords flow as best they can with that missing string, and they connect me to her in this bus that drove her off into the sunset, that remained after she passed. The lyrics pass by in my mind's eye.

Your eyes a scarlet letter, your hands a starlet's dream,
Took a while, took some time, for us to be you and me,
You were the songs before you knew it,
The memories before they were mine,
And I think I'd take back the seconds,
Every one before you were mine.
That moonlit night you whispered,
Go be the star you're meant to be,
And I whispered back, whispered once,
Baby, please come with me.

The lyrics trail off as tears choke me again, and I hug the instrument to my chest, alone with her despite Edie's presence.

Getting to my feet, I keep the guitar close, and this time the rustle-creak of it is unmistakable. Edie's eyes land on my expression, and there's a tug in my core, a feeling. Setting it down on the dining room table, I reach carefully beneath the strings.

Papers slip under my fingertips, so I pull them out.

Above her guitar, in her tour bus, I hold the next pages.

TORI

1989

Music held its secrets tight. So did musicians. Everyone was too caught up in their own songs to dig into other people's, and our next practice began and ended as usual. Patrick slipped in. Sara sent him a look. Edie whispered something to me I didn't hear. Mateo barely glanced up. And I tracked Patrick's movement. The slope of his shoulders. That tattoo. The lies in the lyrics around him. But I'd decided as long as he kept singing, I could ignore that. I didn't need to ask so long as it didn't affect our music again.

I turned back to the group. Smiled, ready for the hit Sara and I had penned together, turning my gaze to her as she led us in.

Ten minutes until everything started. Ten minutes until everything changed. Beside me, in the mirrors of a tiled bathroom, Sara and Edie finished getting ready. I pinned back two curls with a rose bobby pin, and I looked at them in our reflection.

"What made you want to be a star?" I whispered.

Sara tilted her head. "It was always music. Always. The first time was at a school talent show where I was the closing act."

Edie shifted. "The first time my parents confiscated my guitar. What about you, Tori Rose?"

I turned it over. I knew what made Tori Rose, and I guess that was kind of the same thing. She was the star. "I heard a love story." My moms' was the strongest I'd ever seen. They started this dream.

The silence settled, and we left together, only separating when Sara went to find Mateo. Edie headed to the bar. I lingered but couldn't place the reason why.

The club was karaoke-based but so different from the Horizon. This place had flashing lights. Drunken laughter. The screech of an out-of-tune electric guitar. The exposed ceiling made everything appear towering. Immense. Possible.

My gaze tracked framed posters along the hall, signed by band members. Names I didn't recognize and ones I did. People who got their start here. Who left the ordinary behind. I scanned to see how I fit in. To see if I could, when I would.

David leaned near the door at the back in his tie-dyed T-shirt and cargo shorts, ready to see us perform. Patrick stood a few feet away from him in jeans. No words were exchanged between the two. Patrick had still barely spoken to me, and I wasn't going to crack first.

Just briefly, my reflection caught in the glass that protected the pictures. I was part of it for a moment. Part of that music. Somewhere between the frames, I stopped. Stared at a space with a crooked nail and empty frame. If this song went the way it was supposed to, in five minutes, nothing would be the same.

Three things happened that night:

1. Sara and I introduced our hit to the world.
2. Fate's Travelers made and earned our name.
3. The owner of the karaoke bar asked if we'd ever thought of being on the radio.

Another week melted into spotlights. Static. Stages beneath our feet. An interview with Camille Cross, a popular host at the station the Midnight Star. The radio played the song once, then twice, then three times. Until we heard it in bars. Until we heard it in streets. Until our melodies bled into Music City.

The next party Fate's Travelers went to on Music Row, we arrived as stars. Edie grabbed my and Sara's hands as soon as we entered and pulled us into the masses, twirled us around, clapping and cheering.

Patrick and Mateo lingered behind, looking from us to each other. Chuckling lightly. David was just beyond them, in the doorway (sticking out like a sore thumb in his beachy attire). I slipped back through the gathering crowd to him, a bass beating in my head and heart while flecks of disco light paraded across the floor around us.

"Hey, you just going to stand there?" I nudged him, tangling my fingers with his and tugging him all the way in. "Not like you to sit out of a party."

He shook his head. "I think we both know I wasn't invited." Still, he didn't protest as I brought him deeper into the noise.

"When has that stopped us before? Besides, no one's invited to these things."

"Your moms called. While you were at practice."

I glanced back at him and the oddly serious expression he wore. "I'll call them when I get back."

"You said that yesterday."

"So?"

"You know, you promised. When we left. To call them, I mean." That didn't sound like what he meant. That didn't look like what he meant from the way he pulled his hand back and stuffed it into his pocket.

Searching his face, I found what I'd always found. Safety. Reassurance. My best friend. But there was something else beneath it. Did he see the way my heart clenched when I thought of leaving Music City and fulfilling the second half of the road trip I'd claimed we were on? His eyes dared me to come out and say it. But I didn't.

I couldn't.

I didn't know what to say.

"I'll call them." I gave my most honest smile, and he seemed to accept it. I'd call them. I would.

Across the room, my gaze met with blue eyes that were studying me and David under the spotlights. Patrick Rose.

"How's your play?" I asked David, turning back to him, having to shout it to be heard.

He gave a thumbs up and left it at that. I couldn't deal with two brooding boys and the unspoken things they were upset over, so I shrugged away. Headed for the alcohol. Edie was monopolizing the bar, taking shot after shot and waving my way.

"Toriiii," she slurred. "My best friend."

I laughed and slid onto the stool next to her. "Do you know what Patrick's problem is?" I knew she wouldn't.

Winking, she nudged my arm. "Always thought that was you." She was too far gone to the booze and the beat to be any help, so I got up to ask Patrick himself. He was too removed. This was starting to really affect the band, not just him, and that was where I drew the line.

"What's that?" Edie asked from behind me. She reached forward, going to touch my guitar, and I swatted her hand.

"Sorry," I laughed. "No one touches my guitar." I swung it around to my front, and right where she'd been motioning, a crumpled paper lay folded between the strings.

"Someone had to touch it." She nodded toward the note I was staring at.

The music froze inside my chest as I unfolded lyrics. Dedicated to me.

She was a shooting star, a blink-of-an-eye kind of wonder,
A blink-and-you-miss it kind of falling fast and hard,
A midnight whisper, a reckless laugh, you knew just then,
From the first notes of her guitar.
This rush, this music was a sin on a Sunday morning,
You'd never hear another song quite like her,
And you knew, you knew right then and there,
You'd fallen for the music of this girl.

Holding the paper to my heart, I looked up, and the boy with the rose tattoo was already staring at me across the room, making his way toward me. My own white-lace dress whipped in the nighttime breeze, a veil of the summer wind fluttering overhead, sneaking through the open door. His eyes didn't leave mine. Maybe he was ready to give some answers after all.

"HEAD FOREVER TO YOUR DREAMS"

Teaser single from Tori Rose's 1996 album Mirror, Mirror

MIA

The train begins and ends in town, but it's always taken me on a journey. Fate's Express is another tribute to my mom. Once an empty railroad that she described walking along the tracks of while searching for adventure—a memory shared in a video interview from thirty years ago—today it's a real train around the outside of Sunset Cove. Pink sides, silver wheels, polished tracks with each car dedicated to a different Tori Rose album.

It's where Britt and my grad class came after prom—when I went with Jess and she went with Angela and we ended up in the *Regret You* car together, a little tipsy and a little close. The night we made our decision to end our slipups, saying number seven would be the last one.

Standing in line with her now, I study the lyrics on the blue envelope. This time, I'm sure. The lyrics are those same ones painted across the wall of my former nursery. There's only one place they could point.

There was a signpost by the crossroads that said 'head
    forever to your dreams,'
But, love, I don't think this was quite what at first it
    seemed,
For my dreams have turned to nightmares, and they're
    haunted by you,
So it's at night I run from dreams, I run from memories
    of you.

When I look up, the tracks sit lonely, waiting for the train
to come back around. The station offers rides every Monday
through Wednesday, and we're catching the last trip of the day.

Tourists—some I recognize from the inn—are posing in
front of another rotting Sunset Cove monument which is the
only thing in this area that hasn't been remodeled. It's a sign
with that phrase on it. It's the inspiration of my mother's song,
carved into wood by whoever first built a station here before it
was destroyed, before it was remade in her memory.

Head forever to your dreams.

"You should open the next envelope," Britt says. "See what
we're looking for."

The past slips away with her voice, and I open it, pulling
out the folded stationery, too used to my mother's writing and
stories after too short a time.

Mia,
    So you've met my best band friend, you've been to a
club, you've seen the vessel of my music, you've found the
meaning of your name.
    Today, I hope you can have a good ride. I hope you
know how much I wish I could be with you. After the
train returns to the station, remember one thing. They say

X marks the spot, but I always believed the music did a much better job.

Love,

Mom

I reread that one line, committing it to memory for the nights when Britt and Lost Girls will be gone. *I hope you know how much I wish I could be with you.*

For a second, it feels like she is.

There's a clacking along the rails, from the direction of the sea, and the train comes speeding our way, slowing and ultimately stopping to let people unload in front of pink velvet ropes. The ticket line moves forward, and we find our way to the front of it.

"Names?" A bored lady with silver hair and a denim jacket scribbles something on a Post-it.

"Britt Garcia."

"Mia Peters."

Her gaze rises to mine. When her eyes widen a little, I sink into myself.

The lady beckons us forward. "You can go."

I reach into my purse, grabbing my wallet. "How much are two tickets?"

"Girl, go on. Next!"

A man who looks to be in his forties or fifties steps forward, muttering something to the woman that makes her laugh.

Britt tugs me forward, grip tight, not in a pressured way but a reaffirming one. We climb the metal steps of the now-empty locomotive, and no specified number of trips will prepare me for this attraction.

It's far from an ordinary train with its throw pillows, couches, band posters, record players, album covers. We head through the cars, and with that her music: *Once Upon an I Told You So* with its lipstick-stained wallpaper and faux wine spills on the white couches; *Forest in the Sea* with its aqua tiles and Polaroids; *Bittersweet Beginnings* with its shattered disco ball and kaleidoscope walls; *That Summer* with its numerous clocks and beach towels; all the way to *Mirror, Mirror* lined with pink caution tape, silver heels, and mirrors on every available space. There are only two albums past this—*How Many Seconds in Eternity?* And *Regret You*—but we stop here because this is the one "Head Forever to Your Dreams" is from.

It gleams, light bouncing off each reflective surface, as Britt and I stand at the entrance. It's the least popular car next to *Regret You*, the latter because people think it's cursed with how she died on that tour, and the former because no one really likes to look themselves in the eye like these mirrored walls force us to.

Britt stops me before I step in, turns me to face her. "Mia?"

"Yeah?" Eighteen years in, I should've learned how to control my heartbeat around her, especially as these four days threaten to become three with a single night.

She takes a deep breath, squares her shoulders. "When I look at you, I see Mia Peters." It's all she says, but somehow that *I see you* feels a million times better than *I love you*. She says it so certainly, in the way that dares someone to tell her she's wrong, and I'm rooted in place as more passengers load the cars we left.

She breaks first for once, willingly, and she's looking at my lips and I'm looking at hers and there are four days until she goes away, but she steps forward and I do too.

We're a breath apart, and her index finger traces my jaw. "We said we wouldn't do this."

I nod. I should back away in the name of sanity, but Edie's words from earlier come back. My mother was taken from me, from us, and no matter what she did, that would have been the outcome, no matter where she went. Some things are inevitable. Night falls, the sun rises, one day the world will end, in four days Britt will leave, but Tori Rose lived in the meantime, and I want that. My treacherous heart wants to *live*.

"We never were very good with rules," Britt adds, and her brow arches, leaving it up to me.

"The music's in the living," I say, pulse racing. "Four days." Whatever comes next, we have this time left together.

"Let's make goodbye our encore?" she teases, and there's something I've never thought of, but before it even fully hits, her lips are on mine and mine are on hers, and my world narrows into the softness, the surety, the wonder of her.

We find our way to a bench so we're not completely blocking the doorway and fall onto the seat. We don't stop for even a moment. It's the last ride of the day and less busy and people avoid the final cars and, well, the whole world could be watching and I could tune it out as long as Britt keeps kissing me.

There's an urgency to our motions. It's been too long, and not long enough to recover from the mess we make together. I angle forward to kiss the lingering glitter along her eyelids, cheeks, forehead, like star-born freckles, and come undone when her lips find my neck.

Her nose nudges mine, and our lips meet again, fingers tangling deeper in hair and hearts on sleeves. We burst and we break. We are dichotomies and paradoxes and lies and happily never afters. We are an ending that wants to be a beginning and a beginning that never got to start quite right. We are everything, and she is everything, and only I know that I truly wish I could go with her.

I wish I could go with her.

We break apart, and I study her eyes, and I let those words settle within me, trying to figure out how I feel about that, about everything. "Thank you," I whisper.

At some point, the train started moving, and the town I've memorized like the back of my own hand blurs by. I want to ask if she thinks us being together one last time before she leaves is going to make it harder, but everything about it is hard, and this is the first thing that's felt good outside of the hunt this whole week.

I note she's studying the caution tape that's so similar to what surrounds the lighthouse in everything except color, but she's also sneaking looks at me in between, the same smug smile on her lips. I can't help smiling back, and she extends her hand to me, palm facing the ceiling. I take it, lacing my fingers through hers.

Silence settles between us as the train gains speed, but it's not uncomfortable, it's just . . . quiet. I think finding someone to be quiet with, just exist with, and still feel better within their presence than without is underrated. It's never the rush or thrill captured in songs, but it's what draws me to her most.

"Could the next pages be at the sign back at the station? The *head forever to your dreams* one," Britt asks when we pass where Back to Me & You sits between the trees, with the tour bus resting invisibly in the forest. I still need to tell her about that find. "That matches the type of place she said to look in the letter."

I nod. "Yeah, that makes sense. I should've checked while we were there." Except there were people posing with her stories. "So I guess we just enjoy the view for now?"

"Sounds good."

And we do. I recount what happened with Edie, whisper it to her as the train ride becomes a mixture of memories strung up somewhere in the space between us. Thirty minutes later, her head on my shoulder and mine resting against her head, the lurch of the train slowing sends us both swaying forward.

Britt gets to her feet before it even stops. "Want to wait here and look? I'll check the sign."

"Sure." I watch her leave.

Outside, more people gather and Britt slips through. I stare at the many mirrors, at my own eyes that look like Tori Rose's. I'm frozen, always unsure if I'm going to be able to leave her.

Getting to my feet, I look beneath the bench, feel around, just narrowly missing where someone decided to stick their gum. Nothing.

"Mia?" Britt makes her way back, shaking her head. "It's not behind the sign."

"Maybe it's not in this car?" I shift to the caution tape, but it only bars a light switch and the wall.

I catch my image in each mirror as I walk by, and then I stop to stare into the last one on that wall, which is framed in carved wood, painted red. But it's not the frame that gives me pause, it's that there's something reflected that I didn't expect: the sign Britt just checked outside, tall enough that its reflection fills the mirror through the window, right as the train finishes unloading and *that song* comes on over the speakers. They always play "Head Forever to Your Dreams" at the end of every ride.

The music marks the spot.

Stepping across the room and avoiding staged heels and cowgirl boots, I feel behind the ornate red frame. Covered by the mirror is a latch, and it slips open to reveal a bundle of pages.

TORI

1989

Fate's Travelers left before the party ended. We let Music City miss us, and we sat together on the veranda of Sara and Mateo's blue house. Sara brought her keyboard out and lounged on the swing next to Mateo, playing "Once Upon an I Told You So." He tapped his drumsticks against the armrest. Patrick and I were side by side on the love seat, and we sang harmonies to match, him warming up to everything since we sat down. Edie sprawled at my feet, back against my legs with her guitar. Twinkling paper lanterns swung in the wind over our heads.

New choruses wound around old ones. Riffs and humming, and then yawns and stretching as the hours wore on.

Mateo sighed after a while, shifting and then standing. "I'm going to turn in. Sara, you coming?"

"In a minute." The notes falling from Sara's fingertips crescendoed.

Edie got to her feet, leaning heavily on me and making me giggle. "See you all later." She patted my head and hopped down from the porch, into the night.

"See you," I whispered. Somewhere in the distance, wind chimes rang as we disbanded.

"Turn the lanterns out when you leave." Sara got up and went inside without another word. Me and Patrick remained on the porch.

"You're quiet," I said to him when the front door shut again. I needed to know why he'd closed off. Those lyrics Edie found in my guitar played on loop inside me, tucked within my blouse as close to my heart as they could get.

His curls swung over his shoulders as he ducked. "I know I haven't been . . . what I promised."

"Why's that? What's going *on?* You told me we were chasing this together."

He looked at me, and those poet's eyes were singing. "You didn't need me to write that song. That hit. How together are we?"

"You *wouldn't* write it. You never came that day in the park. You asked me to follow the music, and you hid without an explanation." My voice rose with each word. "Sara wasn't scared. You were."

"Tori . . ."

"What?"

"I'm sorry."

It hung there for a moment. His gaze was earnest. His lips formed another silent apology. Lyrics spanned the space between us, but I didn't sing them.

I reached out, and my nail traced across the lines of his tattoo. The falling petals. The thorns. So intricate. Beautiful. Dangerous. "What happened to the boy who interrupted my song and asked me to follow the music? I'm still the girl who interrupted you."

He clasped my other hand to his chest. "I'm still here. I want to be here."

"Where's it from?"

"Where's what from?"

"Your tattoo." I hoped the answer to my question could start him on the truth and make him tell me why he disappeared, why he'd pouted ever since.

His eyes sparkled. He shifted again so that I could see it in all its full, bewildering glory. And then he sat crisscross on the love seat. He faced me. I did the same, and our knees met in the center. The skin-to-skin contact set me on fire in a way that had me imagining just how fast he could make me burn. The note hummed against my skin.

"You like it?" he asked.

"It's why I talked to you in the first place . . . it's why I sang with you."

"Really?"

"Yeah. It's hot."

He laughed. "I designed it myself."

"A secret artist?" I quirked a brow.

"Love, I don't think that's ever been a secret." His wink had my toes curling.

Love?

"So tell me the story of it. All songs are a story. Tell me yours."

He sighed. "It was a stupid fucking decision."

"The best ones are."

Another laugh. "Yeah, okay. So one of my friends back home bought a tattoo gun. She wanted to be a tattoo artist and all. She was great. I swear she graffitied half our town. She wanted to put her mark on everything. She told us she couldn't be remembered otherwise. Once when she was drunk and I was walking her home, she said *she* couldn't remember otherwise. I guess she wouldn't let herself. That night she made us sit in this, like, cultlike circle on her deck overlooking the beach, and we passed that tattoo gun around. And then she raised it and said *Who's first?*"

"*Oh.* Damn."

"Tell me about it. Anyway, most of the group backed away. One dude did a full-on crab walk out of the circle. I stepped forward. I remember her looking at me, and she had that artist's look in her eyes. You know it?"

This was why I came with him.

I nodded. "I do."

He smiled in that daring way again and said, "I sat in front of her on the deck. We were close back then, and I could feel her hand shaking, so I grabbed it and I said *I trust you*. Maybe it helped. She told me to tell her what I wanted. And it hit me. It's kind of an addicting pain. Both the tattoo and the dream. I don't know, Tori. We were lost and ambitious, and we branded our wildest dreams on our skin that night. All of us. It was like some promise. No matter how far we went, we had that night."

"That's beautiful, Patrick Rose."

"Says you," he breathed. There was a pause between us about eight beats long before he added, "There are music notes in it."

"What?" I froze.

He cleared his throat and rubbed a hand along the back of his neck. "In the petals. There are music notes. They're the chords to 'Don't Stop Believin'.'"

"What is it with you and that song?"

His eyes grew sad, and I knew he was about to tell me. I inched closer.

He opened up. "It reminds me of home. Before my parents sent me to Sunset Cove. Before my grandpa there kicked me out. My friends and I would play Journey everywhere. It was our soundtrack to life, really. My parents lived and breathed music in a way. I thought that maybe I was doomed to it from the start, either by breathing it in or choking on their carbon dioxide. But it wasn't all music they liked. They were Journey enthusiasts.

That was all they listened to. My dad worked in the garage a lot. He basically lived there. I'd go out just to spend time with him. We wouldn't talk, but the only time he was proud of my voice was when I sang Journey songs. Only way we connected. Parents didn't believe in me or my own songs, thought the ones I wrote were a waste, but they believed in that music and that band. Practically made it a fucking religion."

"I believe in you." I said. I didn't hesitate. At least that explained his love of covers. His fear. I understood a little better. "I believe in your music. You just have to give it a chance. Like you gave us. Can I take a closer look at your tattoo?"

He nodded, but he didn't say a word. Sweeping his hair off his neck, I traced the outlines of the artwork. The ink had long ago bled into his skin. I suddenly wanted this, a brand like that (from the dream). A way that it'd always be part of me. When I slept. When I was old and gray. When I was six feet under. There would always be melodies on my skin.

Sure enough, there were music notes engraved in the rose that marked him. They trailed along the winding staff within the petals. I followed them with my fingertips, and Patrick sucked in a breath.

"Tori . . ." he said again.

My lips hovered above his skin, and I kissed the ink there. I whispered against it. "You're going to write a song with me. Tonight. I'm going to teach you how to believe in your music. We're going to get everything you promised."

"I *can't*."

"You *can*."

He had to. We had to keep the music going between us. The lyrics he wrote screamed his potential and talent. Sitting behind him, still tracing his tattoo under the porch lights, I whisper-sang to him to prove this.

In the town where the sunset lingered with ocean waves,
Lived a hopeless girl who forgot to behave,
And when she was young her mamas told her 'bout
*   destiny.*
They said: baby girl, go be who you're gonna be,
But when the sun starts to rise don't you forget to come
*   home, don't forget you,*
For the songs in that heart or the devil-may-care tune.

With the rush of the sea the girl found her escape,
She found her way out of the lighthouse's reign
In a rose-painted boy who was brought in by fate.
And it was on that same forever-tinted beach,
The boy said to girl come follow the music with me.

And the songs in my heart won't be silenced by dawn,
Because honey the music's been raging too long.
So in this garden of dreams, constellations at its seams,
I ask you this time: will you follow the music with me?

Patrick just looked at me when I finished. His mouth slowly swooped closer to mine. This boy, this musician, wasn't a danger to my drifter heart or my dream. He was a wolf in a cautionary tale. The heartbreak hidden within a verse. A lie spoken right before the truth came out. And I wanted to discover him because he wasn't a threat at all. Not the way David had always been. Better yet, that verse he'd left on my guitar showed he got me. I leaned in too.

When we were a breath apart, I said, "Thank you for the lyrics."

His lips nearly brushed mine. "What lyrics?"

I pulled back. "What do you mean? The ones in my guitar." My heart hammered. The rush of reading those words that seemed to understand me so completely came to the forefront. Their writer fell for me as I was.

Patrick rubbed a hand over his forehead. "Tori, I . . . I told you I gave up on my own songs. I thought when I got here, they'd just come, but I didn't write you anything. I wish I had, but I didn't . . ."

"That's impossible. You were coming around. You were telling me . . ."

I didn't write you anything. Those words circled in his blue irises as his brows furrowed in this spinning night. It hit. The kiss faded from my mind. I moved farther back on the loveseat as forest green eyes seared behind my vision.

Patrick hadn't written those words. He hadn't captured me in a song.

But I knew who had.

"H(OUR)GLASS"

From Tori Rose's 1998 album
How Many Seconds in Eternity?

MIA

"It has to be David, right?" I lean backward on Britt's bed, head next to the end of the mattress while she's curled against the headboard, tuning her guitar. "My dad. It has to be him . . . if Patrick didn't write that song."

"I mean, there were *years* between that and when you were born, Mi." She swipes something on her tuning app, strumming a chord and adjusting the top peg again.

"True." I shake my head. My mom was in her thirties when she had me. She's only eighteen in these pages. Anything could've happened in that time, but she's also here helping me piece things together, so I have to believe the answers are present, somewhere. We're so close. And it feels like . . . it feels like she might be giving me a green light, saying, *Go.* "Do you think he's the one she writes her songs about though? *Regret You* . . . I've always wondered."

"Me too," Britt says, fingers finding G major. "He could be. He definitely could be . . . I wouldn't want that."

"What?"

She shifts a little closer, and I sit up. "To have a whole album full of regrets."

My next inhale is sharp. The way Britt says it is so simple, so clear. Her brown eyes scan my features, and my cheeks heat under the intensity of her stare.

And that look she gave me when I was just *honest* on the train has me saying, "I wrote all the songs about you."

She takes me in a second, smile starting slow and falling just as easily. She nudges me. "What a silly thing to do." But her voice is choked. She blinks a little too fast. Some calculation passes behind her eyes. "I have something for you."

"Oh yeah?"

Crossing her legs again, she faces me fully, reaching for her guitar once more. "I wanted to play you a song."

I expect her to play it here, the two of us curled up on her covers, but she gets to her feet. Her hair is tossed up in a bun, her face is scrubbed clean of makeup. She's wearing an oversized green sweatshirt, and she's a star but she's also just a girl—she's a galaxy but she's also this huge piece of my world.

Fingers finding my wrist gently, she leads me out of her room, to the middle of the narrow hallway. The stairs stretch one way, and at the bottom of them, murmurs can be heard from her parents' midnight conversations. Across from the stairs, two glass doors lead to a small porch. We walk out into the night air onto the same patio we've been so many times. The beach rests below on either side of us, and homes line the edge of it.

"Britt . . . what are we doing?"

"Trust me." Her gaze looks like it did when she asked if I'd ever said *fuck caution.*

She knows I trust her. I follow her onto the railing of the porch, and we climb atop it, sit, swing our legs. We could fall so easily but we don't. In the distance, the sea and stars mingle, and I breathe it in from what momentarily feels like the edge of the world, here with her.

Smiling at the view, she reaches out like she can grasp the horizon. "I love it out here. Mile said they wanted to see the stars every night. Dania said she needed to be in proximity to the sea. This is the best of both worlds." Britt's expression is loving as she speaks of her parents and this house she's driving off from soon. She's going to have both too—a love for here and an adventure there.

"Why are we out here?" I ask.

She looks at me, serious and open. Her lips are rising into a smirk, and her chin lifts ever so slightly. "The music's what you make it."

The town rushes under us with those words. Sitting there, she pulls her guitar closer one more time, and she sings.

> *I always told you I was leaving, and hon I said I had a place for you.*
> *We were never something to believe in, but you gave me something true,*
> *A penny for the wishing well, and a penny for your thoughts,*
> *Forever's a hell of a promise, and babe we know we're not.*
> *This town has all our memories, and this town contains your world.*
> *I need an open road adventure, I'm wandering a spirit, a restless girl.*
> *I have histories to discover and futures to create.*
> *I have songs to tell my stories, but I hope this one's not too late.*
> *I had the best of years with you, and in memories I'll recall,*

*The way your hand looked in mine, the way this sunset
shaped us all.*
*I know our story's over now, but we've each got a next
chapter ahead,*
*Really, what I want to say, is sometimes goodbye's not
the only end.*

The last chords finish, and the night envelops us.

"You wrote me a song," I say. I'm breathless, and there are no more words. The song is upbeat, raw, juxtaposing the careful nature of everything she said. How did I ever hide this, hide *from* these feelings for her? Did I ever?

Britt's hand moves closer to mine. "I'm glad I knew you, Mia Peters."

"I'm glad I know you, Britt Garcia. Go show the world your galaxy."

There are just two envelopes left—one indigo and one violet. They shake in my hands where I'm standing out in the inn's parking lot, just a couple steps from walking inside. I could slip my nail under the lip of them and *know*. I could read the clues and use them to help me find the next places faster, working backward instead of forward.

I could peek ahead.

Four days will be three in just a few hours, and now more than ever, I need to know Tori Rose's story so I can start my own off right. I need to know what happened in the end.

Britt's song still playing in my ears, I finger the lip of the indigo envelope. I could do it.

But the words from that first page still me. *I promise it'll make so much more sense if you do it one by one.* She asked me to wait, she asked me to do this right, and when she's never asked anything of me before, how can I break that unsung promise? Am I really ready for this to be over, as much as I have to know what to do next?

Slipping the envelopes back into my purse, I don't walk inside just yet. I head over to my bike and clasp that rose charm. I won't let her down, I'll do this just as she wanted. There's still one other way to figure out fast just how much the music calls me.

Through the glass rooftop, Back to Me & You is flushed in the impending cosmos and the still-darkening sky. It's only ten o'clock, the very same day Britt and I kissed, Edie showed me the tour bus, Britt played me her song, but it feels like it's been an era. There's only an hour left until my curfew.

Four days are becoming three.

In my hand, I hold my mother's guitar, which I've skirted around and admired ever since Edie handed it to me and I played that single song on her tour bus. I stand at the edge of the crowd, waiting my turn.

I have to know. The signs seem to point in this direction so far, my mother seems to indicate it, and it's selfish, so selfish, but I need to know if the consideration is worth it. I have to know what would happen, just how much the melodies can call me if I let them.

"Returning so soon?" An unusually cheery voice comes from behind me, and I turn to face Edie. Her purple hair is clipped back with sparkly silver pins, and her jacket is red tonight. What happened on the tour bus lessens the tension between us until this is just my mother's friend and I am just my mother's daughter.

"I thought I wouldn't run away this time," I say but the lightness I aim for is razor-sharp because I've spent my whole life running.

"Do you sing like her too?" Edie asks, balancing a tray of empty glasses on her hip, and I remember humming for her, playing for her, but now I'm going to cross that line. The way she says it is no longer an expectation, it's a dare, to sing a song and go my own way too.

It's a challenge I'd like to meet, and so I pull old lyrics from my back pocket, the ones from the songbook I buried beneath old textbooks before I banished myself to just chords.

Edie leaves it at that, and with each passing singer, I get closer to the stage. I have to know, have to figure this out, have to give it one last chance, give the music one final word in this as to whether or not I can be happy *here*.

When it's my turn to step up to the stage, I do so cautiously, and I purposefully study that poster of my mother in the window on my way up. When I go to adjust the microphone, it screeches, and maybe that's a sign too, but I ignore it.

I steel my shoulders like Britt did, position myself center stage like my mom would, but when I speak it's all me, trembling, aching, *doing this*. "Hi, my name's Mia. This song is called 'Tomorrow's Problems.'"

It's the first song I've performed that's just my own, and all those years of not singing collapse, like it's been no time at all. My fingers find frets, find their homes along the strings, and I hum low into the mic before I let the music out.

I can't count the times I've wanted to kiss you but don't
'cause you're not mine,

*But let's steal a moment, steal just one, beneath the
  shadows of this night,*
*And come with me, down this street of dreams, inhibi-
  tions shed in waves,*
*We'll put this night on tomorrow's dime, see if it stays
  when sunrise fades.*

*I'll wish on stars and empty things, pretend the sky can
  give us hope,*
I'll promise we'll last forever in a way I know we won't,
*We're our whispered oaths, our borrowed time, and a
  lost love letter,*
*But tonight we're flying, no looking down, maybe to-
  morrow we'll be better.*

I love yous are a lie, and almost is our word,
We're a star-crossed second chance wasted in this world.
*We're a promise left shattered as the memory finally
  fades,*
*That's what happens to a photo when you leave it in the
  rain,*
*And I know that this will end, we're playing a win-less
  game,*
*But tomorrow's problems feel so good when I can be
  with you today.*

When the last words fall, I stand before the crowd as the
clapping starts. Expressions change between spotlights, and my
heart races under watchful eyes, waiting for the lights, the com-
parison, shouts about Tori Rose. My hands shake, grasping the
guitar, but when a whistle rings out from somewhere near the
back, I raise my mic and tip my head back. I honor her on my

own terms, and everyone goes wild. Somewhere in the hazy light is Edie, and I know now what the dream really means.

I wanted and never wanted it to feel this good, but now I know.

Here in this club, in my song, in my revelation, I might look like Tori Rose, but I sing like Mia Peters.

MIA

I slip into my room through the window, landing with my mother's guitar at my side. Its roses twist around me, steal my heart. I just played this guitar once held by Tori Rose that has nearly as many legends as she does, and I made it my own. I made our intertwining stories my own.

Breathless, I'm flushed in the applause of the stage and the memories of Edie and my words afterward across the bar, with me sitting on one side and her polishing wineglasses on the other. We talked under the night sky and fluorescent lights that loom over Back to Me & You.

"Wow, you . . . can sing, kid."

"Thanks."

"She'd be proud. I wish she could've seen that."

"Me too."

I set her guitar on the hanging chair, beneath the one on the wall that Grams gifted me, and someone clears their throat from across the room.

"So was that her grad gift to you?" Nana.

I spin to my bed where both my grandmothers are sitting, side by side, clutching each other's hands. I wonder if they can see the joy of the stage still dancing across my skin. How I felt there what I always feel singing with Britt, something I'd written off as more about the girl I sing with and what I can't have than the music. But here it is, right in front of me.

I want it. I want the music.

My grandmas look so frail, sitting there before me, aged by their tragedy. *They won't survive it, they won't survive it, they won't survive it.*

Grams stares as Nana's eyes flicker between me and my mother's guitar, and she pats the bed in between them, scooting over to make space.

All across my room are framed pictures of us and other tangible reminders of everything they've done for me. There are the books they bought me, the posters we picked out together, mostly of Taylor Swift accompanied by Tori Rose, ones I grabbed on my own. And then there's that latest framed photo they took of me and Britt at graduation.

And here I stand, wearing an old *Regret You* T-shirt, fresh from singing in her club, with her supposedly lost guitar.

"Mia," Grams says, and I sit between them. "What's going on?"

They're finally asking about her, about the hunt. Why do I wish they hadn't?

"It was part of it," I say, and they each take one of my hands as the stars bleed down on us. They look at her guitar. "She . . . she led me to it."

Grams nods, and Nana sits too still, stricken.

I think back to Britt not wanting an album, an era, full of regrets.

"I'm sorry," I whisper, but I don't want to be. I don't want to regret this too.

"Sweetheart, why are you sorry?" Grams brushes my hair back, giving a shaky smile, and Nana softens too, squeezing my hand.

"Because I'm like her. But I'm also not. I want what she wanted, but I'm also not her. And I know I can't go but—"

"Why can't you go?" Grams asks, and it's like all these years were nothing. But I've *seen* it, seen the pain they face. That wasn't imagined.

"What do you mean?" I shake my head, getting up and pulling my hands away, standing in front of them. "I can't do that to you, not like she did. You need help at the inn, you need me. And she ended in tragedy; why would I follow that path? All anyone cares about is her fame. You couldn't even talk to me about the gift she left, how should I have expected you'd be okay with me following her, following music?"

Nana's voice struggles to stay even, but her expression is gentler, the same as it's been for eighteen years. "Then we should be sorry."

"Mia." Grams reaches forward for my hands again, and I let her. "We wanted to let you find her on your own. We backed off this summer because we didn't want you looking over your shoulder at us. We wanted you to know your mother."

"What about all the times before this summer? You've never wanted me to know her." It comes out too sharp, and it shatters their features, and I hate myself a little more for that.

Grams, the storyteller of the three of us, takes the reins. "It's hard to see so much of her in you, but you're your own person too, Mia. You're your own story. Of course we want you to know her. It's just . . . it's hard to be the ones to tell you. That's not fair, but it's true."

"But you were so relieved when I said I was staying here, going to college, helping at the inn." I gesture faster with each word. All this time and they claim they wanted me to know her? I love them with this entire piece of my heart, but that wasn't clear, it never was.

"Sure we were," Nana says, a careful equation in each of her words. "Selfishly. But not if you're not happy. We let her go, you know." Her voice breaks, and Grams rubs a hand over her back softly. "We'd let you go too."

"But I didn't want to do that to you."

Grams gives the slightest smile. "Really? Or was that the easiest excuse?"

From anyone else, that'd come out harsh, but from her, it settles into every time I've run away. The two of them get to their feet and hug me, and I'm overwhelmed by vanilla and love and years and the women who've raised me.

"We love you, Mia. We want you to be happy. You finish whatever story she left," Grams says as she and Nana cross the room to my door. "And then you tell us your decision."

They leave with only one more backward glance.

My mother showed me the way; they gave me permission. Now all that's left is me.

I settle onto the chair in front of my vanity and pull out my phone. Mom never made an Instagram—it wasn't invented when she died—but her bandmates did. And so did David Summers, but his is private. I've looked at the band's a million times, memorized their feeds.

Edie Davis's account is perpetually inactive with her last photo being a slice of cheesecake from 2011, accompanied by two random pictures of guitars.

Mateo Ramirez, the owner of a large record store in Music City, is constantly posting new song recommendations and pictures of himself with Sara Ellis, his wife of fifteen years, on her tours.

Patrick Rose. His feed is mostly beach pictures, so that narrows his location down to just about anywhere along the coast. In the latest one, he's with a dark-haired woman, sporting a ruby ring. Something about the picture turns my stomach. I don't know if he's *him*, if he or David is my father, but in this, he's moved on. In this, he's no longer caught up on her.

Needing to get away from that image and whatever slew of emotions bombards my heart at the sight of it, I click on to the last member's page, the only one still living the music, who would truly know if it's worth the chance of regrets.

Sara Ellis.

Her profile is a mix of short videos of her in front of the piano, new and rising artists she's supporting, and sunsets. Her bio is her name, a keyboard emoji, and a single line: *music keeps you young.*

Staring a second longer at the album cover that's her profile picture where she's standing before the sunset, I click the message box. Before I can second guess, I type and send.

Today, 11:18 p.m.

@miapeters: hi Sara. My name's Mia Peters, and I'm Tori Rose's daughter. I know you were in a band together. I'm not sure if you'll see this, but I just had to try. She's left me this hunt. It's all these clues that lead around our town and unlock bits of her journey and her story. I've spent my whole life searching for her with so few leads, but her music, my music, is starting to call me with everything she unravels.

My family hasn't been the same since she died. We barely talk about her. Tonight was the first time in years that we have, and they told me to choose my path, to tell them my decision. I know she was sick, I know she made the most of everything and lived her life regardless, but I'm still stuck on how her last album is named Regret You, on how my town remembers her all wrong.

Fate's Travelers meant something to her. You meant something to her, so I'm kind of trying to find anyone who can help me figure out what she was like behind the spotlight, what she'd want to be remembered for. Do you ever regret it? Did any of Fate's Travelers?

I just wanted to message. She told me to follow the music, but I don't know where it's going to lead.

MIA

Three days until Britt leaves. After a night with no sleep, staring at my phone, hoping miraculously Sara would see my message and reply, I know I need to choose. For real. Because once I do, I don't want to go back: that'll be my future.

All morning while I work the desk of the inn, organizing drawers to keep my fidgeting hands busy until I can leave and search more, I feel my grandmas' eyes on me, waiting for me. I want the music, I love it; I want Britt, I want to be with her, but will that be enough in the end? I finally know that the music didn't destroy my mother. I could make my own path, but after a lifetime hiding from it, how do I say I'm ready?

I still need to know her ending.

The indigo envelope beckons, and I open the bottom drawer of the desk, pulling harder when it sticks. Inside, buried beneath old invoices that I toss toward the shredder, a playbill pokes out, faded. It's from a Sunset Cove rendition of *Grease* in 1989. How long has it been since these drawers were cleaned?

But as I pull it out and flip through it, a familiar face smiles at me, eyes on something other than the camera. David Summers. This was *that* summer, the summer they left for Nashville and New York, and he's Danny Zuko. So they came back after. He and my mother came back from their Summer of Dreams, even if only for a while.

I shove the playbill away with the envelope and recite the lyrics of this clue to myself.

> *I've always been center stage, asked the limelight to bring me home,*
> *When I saw you up there, your turn to shine, the undeniable star of the show,*
> *I couldn't help the awe on my lips or the way my hands applaud,*
> *Our future seemed unending, for I loved everything I saw,*
> *Who knew the beginning of us would end with a curtain call,*
> *Who knew the lies between us would be broken by the truth,*
> *And the night right here before us would be the final act of me and you?*

The Sunrise Theater is at the edge of Sunset Cove with the waves crashing over the sandy shore just beyond it. Linnea told us years ago that this building used to be the beating heart of town. Now, all it's got to show for itself is sea-stained siding and a door that creaks.

Britt and I duck inside, into the lobby with its worn floor

and framed playbills stretching down the hall. From 1980 to 1989, David Summers stands center stage in all of them.

"Can I help you?"

The same guy who's always here sits behind the front desk. He's the kind of town legend that isn't shared, that fades into the background to go unnoticed. Haunting the theater day in and day out with his gray hair and gray shirts that make him look like he had the life sucked out of him.

Yet, no one really questions this or the fact that productions are as rare as snow. This building is more fond memory than anything else, another monument to what the town was before.

"Which room was the 1989 mainstage production in?" I ask.

His lips purse, and he shuffles some papers around in the clutter of his desk. "Believe that was *Grease* in 3A. Down the hall. Last one at the end."

"Can we check it out?"

He doesn't meet my eyes—like I'm just another poster on these walls. "I have an appointment in an hour. You have until then."

My love,
   Isn't there a magic to the spotlight?

That's it—that's all the contents of the indigo envelope say—and I reread it over and over. Britt's sitting next to me in one of the patched-up red audience chairs, elbows on her knees, head in her hands, eyes flickering between me and the stage.

The theater is a relatively grand room with rows of seating, a tech booth in the back, and spotlights on a catwalk that's anchored to the ceiling. The stage is bordered by red drapes, and a cyclorama stands in the back.

There's not much to make of that one line, especially in the vastness of this room. I pace between the aisles, trailing my fingers across the seats filled with more forgotten history, more lost moments, more painted-over truths. My combat boots click with each step onstage, and I look out at Britt, not used to this perspective.

She's looking at me too, considering, under a wide-brimmed sun hat.

And I need to tell her something, it's filling me, haunting me, so I say, "Would you sing with me?" The words tremble, but they're there.

Her eyes widen, but after a moment, she gets to her feet, heading to the stage to join me. She crosses this room with all its inactive spotlights and empty promises. Stopping next to me, she stills, and we both stare out at the crowd for a moment.

And I start to sing to her. I give her a song. Every lyric was shaped in her name, and it's the first melody of mine she knows is hers.

> *Star-born wonders and racing hearts,*
> *Your hand in mine and the blue, blue sky,*
> *An adventure nowhere and ticket everywhere,*
> *Tangled falsehoods keeping us alive,*
> *You've got my destination in your heart,*
> *One arm out the window and a hand on the wheel,*
> *Baby I promise you and this almost-open-road*
> *   adventure,*
> *I'd give everything to make us real.*

She twirls toward me and takes the reins, continues the tune so effortlessly it has my brain spinning even worse than when her lips were on mine.

Mysteries and madness, in a summer that steals our fate,
Never did believe in destiny, but this one's worth the
      wait,
I'd follow you if I could, I'd be right there, be right
      here,
If goodbye's in our cards there's one thing you need to
      hear,

If I could I'd tip the scales, if I could I'd buy the world,
For a chance with you, to make us real, to join the mu-
      sic of your world,
Make us real, oh oh oh,
Anything to make us real.

Britt stares at me, unwavering as my voice ebbs away. The words are on the tip of my tongue, and I just need to push them out. I need to say what I know to be true. But I stand in the center of that stage and look out at the empty audience.

It's just another ghostly place with the lingering monuments of how this town used to be and what it was shaped into in its grief. Grief always shows—it uses the littlest things to make itself known. Like an empty theater and a heart of a town beating no more, covering its faded edges with new relics to act whole, and like a once blazing star, forever preserved but never spoken of in all her realities.

Standing up here, with only Britt Garcia near me, is just as fulfilling as that night in my mother's tribute club. The stage, this girl feels like a new kind of home—like a long-awaited journey.

"Spotlight," Britt says to herself in the silence, and then to me.

"What?" She's so close. *Say it.*

"The song is 'See You in the Spotlight.' How could we

possibly continue without one?" Her smile could get me to do anything—*Fuck caution.*

"So," I say, and her gaze is testing me. "Let's get one."

"I like that plan."

My stomach flutters.

We hop to the floor and make our way through the seats. The tech booth at the back is slightly newer than the rest of the place, but an old ladder with more dust than stability leads to the catwalk and the lights mounted there.

Taking it one rung at a time, a different vantage point is created. My fingers trail along the rail when we reach the top, and in my mind's eye, this room is filled with people. I can visualize Britt and I standing there just as we were, singing with Lost Girls. I can picture us all visiting Sunset Cove, performing in Back to Me & You, crowding into a car, and driving with pitstops and laughter through the sunset, all the way to Music City. I can imagine me and Britt, on the steps of the Grand Ole Opry, walking the line of Music Row, at parties, forever in the melodies.

There are three spotlights up here that clearly haven't been used in years. I was stage manager for a couple of school productions Britt starred in, so I have a basic understanding of this technology, and I turn each one on—one at a time, illuminating different parts of the stage with golden light. One, two . . .

On the third and final one, something slips beneath my hand as I brush dust from the surface. My palm smooths over a pack of papers, and I stop, pulling them off the light as best I can to reveal my mother's second-to-last diary pages.

TORI

1989

Patrick remained silent a little too long, so I walked away. I followed those lyrics that bled into me like the ink on his skin. They branded me in a way. A montage of moments took over, and I ran. My feet pounded against the ground. Up the road. Around streetlights. Beneath neon lights. In front of bars that rang out with noise and cheers and past open mic sessions and the comforting thrum of a guitar. Memories followed each movement.

David filled every one.

Us when we were little hanging out in a pillow fort with brooms for lightsabers. Whispering beneath the cover of our built shelters. Falling asleep on his shoulder. Trying a joint his friend handed me. Watching the smoke fly into the sky with my screaming dreams. Racing down the shore alone with him. Crashing into each other and falling to the sand.

I flew up the stairs of the hotel, past the startled man and his vest of the day in the lobby. The door to David's and my room swung open. He was going out as I was going in.

"David," I breathed, hands on my knees and hair falling in sheets around me.

He scanned behind me, out into the hall. "Someone chasing you?"

"Patrick didn't write that song." His forehead creased, and I reached into my blouse. I handed him the paper.

He didn't look at it. Just passed it back. His gaze was far more closed off than those open-hearted lyrics. *David.* David had written this for me.

"Tori..." he began, and it sounded wrong. He didn't call me *T.* There was an edge to it. My name in his voice ricocheted around us.

Without finishing his sentence, he walked right by me. He moved out the door and into the hall. The rooms were positioned in this rectangular shape, and he wove around to the alcove where they kept the vending machine.

"David!" I called. "Where are you going?" I sped after him, and he stopped to insert some coins. A bag of chips fell out.

I leaned beside him against the counter that contained an old coffee maker and lipstick-stained mugs. In my peripheral vision he was golden hair, long lashes, a goofy patterned shirt.

"What's going on? You just wrote me a *song.* Why did you walk away?"

"Of course you thought it was him." He turned to me. "Of course you *wanted* it to be him." The betrayal in his irises was deeper than I'd ever seen it.

"I didn't *want* it to be him."

"Words and actions say different things."

"They usually do."

"This isn't a joke, Tori." There it was again. *Tori.*

"If it was, I missed the punch line."

His eyes said *I'm the punch line*, and I wanted to tell them to shut up.

"You're always in motion," he said, grabbing the chips and setting them on the counter behind me, busying his hands with getting coffee I knew he wouldn't drink. "I've always admired that about you. But this summer, it was supposed to be *ours*. And he's here, and—"

"He's part of the dream. My dream. This band." *But he walked away from the music.*

"I get that."

"David, I want to be a star. He's part of *that*."

"You're always the star," he said, and it wasn't bitter. It was matter-of-fact.

"I'm sorry," I told David. Meaning it. Not sorry for being the star but that I hurt him.

His Adam's apple dipped. "And you're so alive here. I thought . . . I don't know. That maybe this summer wasn't ours anymore. That you were settled and wouldn't want to go any-where else . . . with me. But I hoped you'd keep your promise for once."

"What do you mean *for once*?" I refused to admit the part of me that had wondered how much this summer was really ours. When the day came to head to New York, I knew I could leave. I *would* leave. But not yet.

Anger sparked in his tone for the very first time. He'd *never* been angry with me. "When do I stop being second place? When do I get to mean as much as *Patrick*? All I've ever wanted was to be there for you, but it's hard when you don't care if I'm here at all. You fall asleep practically on top of me. Sneak into my room back home. We share a *bed* here. You look at me some-times and I think I mean something, and I try to show you how I feel with those lyrics, but . . . you just don't care when it's from me. You thought it was him."

"How can you say that? Of course I care." Tears rose in

my eyes. He was *David*. Good, sweet, thoughtful David from Sunset Cove and neither Tori Rose nor Tori Peters could *ever* stop caring about him.

"Could've fooled me."

"I'm not trying to fool you." I took a step closer. "I didn't know you wrote that song, yes, but you're not second place. I didn't write every song about him. He didn't slide into the lyrics when I was Tori Peters dreaming about being a star. Dreaming about *you*. He wasn't the green-eyed boy I thought of. He wasn't the constant when I was flying everywhere just to be somewhere. Patrick is not who I write my songs about. And where does *that* leave me?"

He stared at me. "I—"

"I care *too* much about you. And that could wreck everything." Tori Peters reared her head inside of me. She stole my tongue to tell him about the girl who once dreamed of him before she dreamed of everyone and everything. He was the only person she trusted with her heart. And the person I trusted least to keep mine a free spirit.

"Tori . . ." He stared at me. And because he was David and no one else, he took my hand, even in his hurt. "It's not Nashville that makes or breaks your gift. It's not Music City that made you a star. It's not the miles between you and that town. It's not forgetting who *you* are to be someone new. The star's inside you, T. She has been all along. Just, please don't make it me or your dream. You can have both. You can."

It sounded so good when he put it like that. It sounded like a new sort of dream. I thought of all those days David listened to my songs. The way he'd joined me this summer with hardly any question. How he came to every show. How he stood, looking at me.

"David," I said, and his eyes were so hopeful. "Can I kiss

you?" Every moment I *almost* had, but hadn't, came back. Those times were ghosts. I didn't want to turn what was between us into something that'd haunt me.

David didn't even nod. He just kissed me. His lips fell open under mine. It was better than flying in truck beds. Jumping off bridges. Gelato on the beach and leaving graduation.

It was almost as good as the music.

His arms wrapped around me, and he spun me so he was leaning into me and I was leaning into the wall. He lifted me, and I wrapped my legs around his hips. His pulse skipped against my chest. My fingers slipped under his shirt, traced the smooth skin of his stomach. He broke for a breath, but then our mouths found each other's again. My hands tunneled into his hair, and I tightened my calves around his hips, tilted my head to get closer. Years of wanting this surfaced in every missed breath.

And for a second, he didn't feel like the past. Not when his fingers were gently tracing over my rib cage. Not when he was holding me like *this*.

Someone cleared their throat.

We both looked over his shoulder at a little old woman. I didn't know what she was doing in Music City, but she was here with a floral nightgown and curlers. She held up a quarter for the vending machine and looked completely scandalized.

I slid down from David's arms.

"You done?" the woman asked.

I glanced at David, and his eyes were *shining*. My smile was ill-kept. The music, if possible, was louder than ever inside me.

"Sorry ma'am." He choked on laughter.

Walking around us, she huffed. David left his chips to take my hand. He breathed the lyrics he'd written for me, and

I wanted every inch of him when he shared them with me. Just that night, I let Tori Peters and Tori Rose collide. My best friend and I ran down the hall, and we lost any composure we had.

When we reached our room, I pressed him up against the door. Held him there with my hands and hips. I kissed the life out of him. We stumbled backward into the room. We fell onto our bed.

And I whispered against his skin, "I never want to regret you."

The next morning, I woke up with my arm across David's bare chest, curled into his side. Smiling at the night before, but knowing the day meant something else. The few inhibitions I had left came thundering back, and they were all about him.

Sunlight danced across his forehead. His verse for me played over and over as I slid out of bed with more care than I'd ever felt. I shuffled into a thin hotel robe and climbed out the window to the rickety balcony where we'd stood that first night.

It cut into my feet, and I stared out at the city that was already awake beneath the dawn in a way that Sunset Cove never had been. I looked back at David, and I thought of New York and then of the town that I *knew* he would one day return to. I knew, if I followed him, I'd be pulled back too.

He'd said it wasn't him or the dream, the past or the future. In the rush and heat of his kiss and those intoxicating lyrics he'd penned in my name, I'd believed him.

But now? Come morning light, I wasn't so sure.

Patrick waited for me in the hall with his guitar. "I'm ready," he said as soon as he saw me. And I knew more than ever the choice that lay ahead.

The night of that performance, the one after which everything changed yet again, I stood with David at a tall table. We laughed as we fought to claim a spot to rest our arms that wasn't laden with sticky beer stains. His breath brushed my cheek as he whispered to me, but I didn't catch the words.

Across the room, the band warmed up. Edie played with the speakers, and Sara leaned against the drum set, talking to Mateo. Patrick was ready to introduce a song he'd written that had only half the heart of the one David had so effortlessly created.

In a minute, I would join them. The pull between a Summer of Dreams with David and *my* dream here tugged at me again, and I knew I had to tell them all the choice I'd made. I remembered how David made me believe everything was right there for the taking.

I turned to him, ready to sink into this performance. This song.

But he was already looking at me.

"What?" I nudged him.

"The play I'm writing," he said softly, and he traced a spot of freckles on my shoulder before kissing each mark on my skin. "It's about a girl and a boy and a Summer of Dreams."

Oh. Oh God.

The mic shrieked up on stage, just like it had the evening Patrick fell into my life at the hands of the universe, and David squeezed my hand.

"David . . ." I trailed off. Fate broke me up inside. Destiny made a fool of my name.

"Tori!" Edie called across a restless bar. "You coming?"

"You can read it after." He smiled a little, and I'd never seen him look shy. "If you want."

"I want," I stumbled over words. "Yes."

"Tori!" Edie hollered with hands cupped around her mouth.

"Coming," I said, as I made my way across the room to the band. Unspoken words now all my own, I cast one last glance at David over my shoulder.

"THE ONE TIME YOU REGRET ME"

Post seven-year release hiatus, from the final album of Tori Rose's career, Regret You

MIA

My mother sees me in these pages, and final pieces snap into place. Tori Rose felt all of this. She felt like I did, stuck between a town that raised her and the road that promised her more.

Except, if I took the road she wanted, the path she desired, I could have the love too. I didn't have to choose like she did. She had choices, she had fears, she had songs that scared her, and she tried her best. She was a million paradoxes, and she wanted the music despite it all. She searched for a way to have it all instead of just accepting she couldn't. And she showed me I could too.

Even with her gone, I'm right here with her, right where she was in these pages. *These pages.*

They're up here for a reason—everything's been for a reason. They have to be attached to this spotlight with a purpose to that location, that has to be a clue of its own, one just beneath my fingertips. I turn the spotlight on, and a glow of brilliant scarlet lands center stage where Britt and I stood minutes before, in the perfect shape of a rose.

"*Britt.*"

"Mia . . ."

This is the sign I've been waiting for.

My mother's light, shaped in her stardom and her name, becomes a beacon.

Britt and I descend the ladder, and I take the first step. I stand under my mother's spotlight and my skin is aglow with roses and full of her promises. Britt's studying me under the same light, and I step toward her. Her eyebrows rise again, but I link our fingers together. She feels right. This feels right. This is it.

"What if this wasn't our encore?" The words release, and my heart hammers, and something within me soars.

Her brows furrow, her lips tip up into a smile. "Meaning?"

"I want to come with you."

Her smile turns to a grin. "You actually said it."

"You were right."

"I know." She brushes a hand over my cheek.

"It doesn't have to be as part of Lost Girls," I continue in a rush. "But I want to get out of here. I want more."

"Nah, you're a Lost Girl." She pulls me closer, taking my other hand in hers. There's no longer a chasm between us, just the music. Forever, the music. "Amy owes me twenty dollars."

"You bet on me?" I laugh.

"Always." She kisses me beneath the red spotlight, on the empty stage, and I sink into her. I let myself.

This is it.

Britt and I only stop to turn the spotlight off, and I whisper a silent *thank you* to my mother somewhere in the celestial sphere. Then, I lace my fingers through Britt's once more, and we run out of the theater, past the quiet man at the front, and through the door. As it falls behind us, the once-heart of Sunset Cove beats again.

We wind up in the cove where we first kissed, swaying in the cold water, half-clothed and giggling.

"This is it," I say aloud this time.

Britt smirks. Under the pull of the salty breeze and dreams, we move toward each other until . . . she splashes me.

Another laugh escapes, and she winks and dives under the sea. She's paddling away, and I'm chasing her, and we're lost in the moment. It might be hours, days, weeks of us here, under the sun with three more days until *we* leave. We splash each other and laugh some more, and it's not so sharp and painful anymore because it's not a goodbye. On that stage, in this ocean, we cross another line, and this is the last one we drew in the sand between us.

When we return to the outcropping of the cove and the alcove it makes, we're shivering head to toe. Fingers wrinkled, hugging ourselves to keep warm, we end up closer to each other. Britt tugs me nearer this time, lifting me, and my legs wrap around her waist as we remain above the shallow waves, her arms slipping under me.

"You're actually coming?" She's breathless, and I don't know if that's from racing around the water or something else.

I nod, arching down to kiss her again.

And finally, finally, *finally*, we don't have to say goodbye.

MIA

Amy's garage is a shrine to the music. All across her walls, there are drummers from Ringo to Viola Smith, singers, pianists, as well as framed lyrics and sheet music. She and Sophie are sitting on a worn, brown couch when Britt and I walk through the door, and both of their eyes jump to me.

"Band meeting," Britt announces, crossing the room and settling on the floor between them, leaning back against the couch. She's so comfortable with them, resting her arms across their knees, and this is what all their practices are like, except I'm not just here working on accompaniments.

Sophie grins at Britt, but Amy's still looking at me, pinning her long black hair up without breaking gaze. Twinkle lights blink overhead in their multicolored hues.

I shift from foot to foot. "Hi."

Britt gives me a look that says *let me do the talking*, so I shut up.

"You remember Mia?" She looks at them both over her shoulder.

"Yes," they both say. Sophie's face is open, welcoming. Amy is more guarded as she leans her elbow against the back of the couch.

"She's coming with us to Nashville. She said she's happy to do the music on her own, but we did give her a week, and I think she'd be a great addition to the band." Britt winks at me, and my heart swells. What did I do to deserve to be with her?

"About time," Sophie says, and her gaze shines.

Amy crosses her arms. "Okay, sing for us. Audition."

Britt laughs. "Ames, you've heard her sing."

"Yeah, in like middle school. Let's hear her again."

My heart calms within my chest at the simple request, the task to earn my place. I sang in the club, I can sing here for a future with Britt and Lost Girls. "Okay, I can do that." I can face the music before I follow it.

Britt gestures to the mic stand across the concrete floor, the one she so often sings at. She walks over and meets me, leaning against the drums in her yellow plaid shirt, tank top, and jean shorts. Her curls are still damp from our dip into the cove, and my ponytail is still dripping icy water down my back.

"You've got this," she says.

"I'll make you proud." I tease, and I lean forward to kiss her cheek because I can. I feel the start of her smile before her mouth captures mine for the millionth time today.

"You'd better." Her words are joking too, but I want to make her proud, I want to do this right, I want to make up for every day I let fear get the best of me.

I pull the mic in front of the couch, and it tangles in the purple shag rug, but I set it in its place. My hands grasp the stand, and I bring it close, hold it like a lifeline. I let the music take me, and after one deep breath, I shift my mother's guitar from my back to my front.

I play.

In this garage with these girls, I sing the very same song I performed that night in Back to Me & You, the song that sparked this change. I let the lyrics unwind, and try to block out the room, the noise of the house beyond the garage, and the street out front. I focus on Britt, and I sing to her.

I let my voice rise and fall. I show them every bit of the musician I want to be. Who Mia Peters is, beyond my mother's guitar, beyond her legacy. There's not a word that says it, not a phrase that confirms this dream. They just get up, and pull me into the music with them, and I've never been more alive.

MIA

When the clock strikes midnight and marks two days left, Britt leans forward and whispers in my ear, "Hey, Lost Girl."

I turn onto my side, curled toward her. "Hi."

We bridge the gap between us, and there's a rhythm to kissing, a pattern, a lyricism that only comes when it's with this one girl. It's a song we perfected long ago, and a tune we practice now, in my room. We rest next to each other on my comforter, legs intertwined, and lips meeting. This is not a countdown; this is not a last kiss. This is a new beginning and, for the first time in my life, that weight forever on my heart lifts all the way off.

Britt shifts so she's over me, sweeping my hair behind my ears. I arch up, kissing her cheek, her neck, her collarbone. Burying her face in my shoulder, she smiles against my skin, and we're at it again. Our words from the stage and the cove brought us here. Our laughs through the dark streets and footsteps through my window and stumbling paces into the house became *this*.

Grams and Nana were having dinner with Dania and Mile,

and so Britt and I had asked to sleep over here. I still need to tell them my choice, but I'm ready. *I'm ready.*

"I'm sorry it took me so long to be sure," I tell her for all the wasted time I spent.

"Stop saying that word. Tell me what you're sure of."

"I'm sure of you." My fingers move to her back, and she squeezes my hips. The kisses get harder, hotter.

"What else?"

"I'm sure I want to follow the music. I'm sure that I want to see something outside this town." She bites down softly on my lip, and I pull her nearer, needing her as badly as I need my next breath.

There's a silence bridged only by the give and take of our lips against each other's, and there are no veiled truths, no almost-lies, no almosts at all.

Britt whisper-sings our songs between kisses. Her humming wraps around us, pulls us into the song, into every one I've written for her and with her and every one that made me think about her too.

Grad night comes back, memories of being behind that stage together, where I'd come from just before that. The words I ran from beat so loud alongside my pulse I'm sure she can hear them already, feel them when she touches me. I've never said them to anyone but my grandmas, swore to myself I never would, but the music is so strong now. The melodies are so much. And she is *everything*.

So I let myself do this, picturing the beach, picturing my head on her shoulder, flying out Jess's window, my cap soaring away. "I'm sure I love you, Britt Garcia." It comes out, tears from the bars of my rib cage, and makes its way between us like it never has before even through all the kissing-in-the-dark, the falling fast and hard, the days and songs together.

She pulls back, and her eyes are wide. It's just the two of

us in the little world of my room, in this roaring moment, and then she's kissing me like she needs me too. "I knew that."

"Oh yeah?" I almost laugh. All this time and she knew. Of course she knew.

"Did you know I love you?" It's said like a challenge—like most of the things she says are—and somehow that breaks and heals me at the same time.

I begin again and again and again. I'm done planning for the end.

"I hoped," I say right as our breaths collide and our lips connect all over and those words become the only thing that matters. "I didn't know. But I hoped so bad."

More and more, we're deepening the kiss. I'm deepening the kiss, and she's deepening the kiss. Suddenly, fingers are reaching for buttons and buttons are loosening and shirts are slipping off one by one.

"Are you sure about this?" she says, pulling my tank top down a little more and pressing her lips to my shoulder.

"I'm so sure." I cup her cheeks in my hands. "I don't think I've ever been surer." Between our kisses—our aching, mesmerizing kisses that wreck me so completely—I whisper against her lips before we go any further, "Are you? Sure?"

"Yes, Mi. I am."

We end up sliding beneath the sheets, clothes slipping off, touch soft and fading, kissing freckles and constellations across one another's skin. We become something we've never been before. Beneath the moonlight and the starlight and the streetlights, I love her so much it consumes me as I whisper everything against her skin and she smooths my hair back and we make promises we can finally keep. She's over me, then I'm over her, and then she's over me again as the digital clock on my nightstand loses the night, time slipping through its grasp. We're tangling fingers in hair and finding something undiscovered in each other and making it so undeniably clear that we made this, *us*, real.

This week might be ending, the open road might be unknown, I may only have one of my mother's clues left, but as the last clothes come off and the last secrets are bared, I've never felt more found than I do here and now with her.

MIA

The last clue of the hunt brings it full circle, and I don't want it to end. At the same time, I'm so ready for the next chapter. Soft melodies play through the earbuds Britt's got in, and I'm close enough to hear them, my head on her chest.

I whisper to her, "I have to do it. I have to finish the hunt. I have to know what she needed to say."

Britt turns to me in the dark where we lay holding each other. "Let's go."

There's only one place the last clue can lead, and I swear tonight's window is the last one I plan to sneak through. But as the sun rises with two days left, I need to finish this if I'm going to leave Sunset Cove behind.

When the ocean makes its leave and the past waves goodbye,

I'm stuck on what we used to be, I'm stuck in broken
    lies,
How we used to talk through tin can-telephones 'bout
    hopes that reached the sky,
How we used to whisper secrets to seashells and walk
    the sand at low tide.
And the betrayal in your eyes was the hardest thing I've
    ever seen,
To read the obituary of your dreams where cause of
    death was 'cause of me.
I realized it was you long after you realized it was me,
    but I chased him still,
And on this beach brushed by smoke and mirrors and
    my glassy tears,
Is the one time you regret me.

It's the bridge of the song that led us to the abandoned house in the first place, marked by that grown-over sign for Miner Lane. It's the same place that led us to the key that unlocked Back to Me & You's fifth door. So we pull up in front of it with those familiar ocean waves.

I take Britt's hand. "Before we do this—"

"Mia," she says, "it's going to be okay."

I take a deep breath. "Thank you." I clasp one of her hands in each of mine like we did on the stage. "Thank you for coming with me and making this the best week of my life. I was terrified of it ending and of losing you, but instead it was *everything* up until the last moment. Thank you for sticking with me even when I made it hard."

She rolls her eyes, but there's a fondness to it. "We don't have a last moment anymore."

I grin, and she smiles right back when I kiss her.

I don't know what comes after the moment you've waited your entire life for, but right now, it just feels like what comes next is my *life*, truly there for me to live.

"I'm ready," I say, and it feels like a mantra at this point.

Britt clicks the button to lock her car as we push open the white picket fence and walk onto the yard, dotted with weeds and wildflowers.

My nails slip beneath the lip of the purple envelope, and I'm about to see the last letter she wrote to me—the last letter she ever wrote as far as I know. The crisp pink stationary crinkles. As much as part of me is desperate to run from another ending and the heartbreak of truly losing her, I stand my ground and I read it aloud.

Dear Mia,

Welcome to my best friend's house. Welcome to the beginning I wish wasn't an ending. Maybe it's not the ending just yet; I don't think I'll ever find out. I wish I was always just a phone call away, but I hope you have this piece of me to hold on to now.

All my love,
Mom

"There are no clues in the letter," I flip over the note, but there's only a line of lyrics, scribbled and crossed out on the back. "I guess all we have is the one that brought us here."

Britt leans closer, taking the note. "She says she wishes she was always a call away, and then the hint talks about telephones. That has to mean something."

"Wouldn't a telephone be inside?"

"Maybe." Britt's already walking toward the house.

"Am I going to have to break and enter?" I ask.

She shakes her head. "We'll save the felonies for Music City."

I catch up to her, and we take in the panels of the house and scratched blue shutters. The ancient door with a broken window. We walk up to a rainbow porch swing and note the initials on the arm of it—*TR + DS were here.*

That day that we skipped class—after we scoured the entire place—we just sat in this spot for hours, talking and playing chopsticks and "two truths and a lie" as the sky faded from blue to pink.

"Do you want to stop for a second?" Britt sits.

I sink into the dusty, worn cushion too and lean my head on her shoulder. "Do you think he still lives here, in this town?"

"Maybe."

"I can't stop wondering if it's him, if he's my dad." This has to be David Summers's former home.

"I don't know, Mi."

"Why did he leave?" I squeeze my eyes shut and tears prick. "Why does everyone leave?"

She squeezes my hand. "I'm not leaving you anymore." She traces a heart on my palm, bringing our intertwined fingers to her lips. "Anyway, you're the one going now."

The swing creaks behind us as we rise, and dust floats into the air. The breeze settles over a set of carvings in the porch's floor.

"What . . ."

Crouching, I trail my fingers across them, and they're guitar chords, engraved into the wood so purposefully, yet worn practically into the surface by time and the elements like the ones on the Horizon's stage. We didn't notice these before. And today, instead of feeling like by bringing her guitar I'm toting her insurmountable legacy, I know I'm carrying every answer I've been seeking.

These chords . . . they're a *trail,* just like this hunt has been.

Britt and I follow them, follow the music etched into the deck, and she whispers the lyrics—because it's a Tori Rose song, a medley really—and we both know it.

At first, it's "Regret You," then "How Many Seconds in Eternity," followed by "Mirror, Mirror," all the way through my mom's career, back to Fate's Travelers' hit "Once Upon an I Told You So." The chords in the floorboards lead all the way to the rear of the house, and the last one is on the railing looking down at a pink rosebush.

I hop down the back steps, and Britt pauses, staying put.

"Mia, look at this." She's crouching, and when I come back to her, she's touching what looks like fishing line, tied to the very bottom of the rail. "I didn't see this last time. It goes through the bush."

"Let me check the other side."

Reaching beneath the bush, I carefully maneuver around the thorns. "Ouch." I don't quite avoid them well enough, but when I feel the other end of the line, it's worth it. Following it with my fingertips, I stop where it goes into the ground, buried beneath.

"It's here."

Britt joins me, and I begin to dig, brushing aside the soil, letting it stick beneath my nails—knowing that in a second I'll have my answers, and in a second she'll be gone all over again. The panic comes quick and hard, and my breaths grow shallow, but I keep going. Every day of my life has led to this, every year, every moment.

This is Tori Rose, and I am her only daughter.

She left this here for me.

When the dirt is cleared, there lies a glint of rusted silver, long ago corroded by the breath of the sea. It's a tin-can telephone.

"Check inside it," Britt says.

I hold up the can and pull out a bundle of plastic-wrapped pages, surprisingly thin. They're without a doubt the end of my mom's diary.

I clutch the final chapter closer to my chest. "Okay, I'm going to read it. Let's finish this."

Britt's arms wrap around my waist, and I lean back, closer to her. As my mother ends, together we begin.

TORI

1991

The spotlights blinded me as I took center stage, and I lifted a hand to shield my eyes. The mic pressed into my palm. I tilted the stand so that the music was barely a kiss away. The beat dropped from behind me, and I met it with a nod and snap of my fingers. Cheers rose before the first words left my lips. I gave my best smile to that crowd made of a couple thousand.

The tattoo on my collarbone caught the gold light that framed me. A rose with only thorns in dripping red. The stem was built from a handful of words: *Go be the star you're gonna be.* From my first country hit to call all my own: "Forest in the Sea." For a second, I forgot the demons that danced with me. The memories that only grew sharper with time. The music was amnesia these days. It was welcomed all the same.

I poured it all into the lyrics, and somewhere out there, my wanderlust reached where it had always wanted to land. I sold my soul to the beat for everything it could demand.

This was everything I'd ever dreamed. I reminded myself of that. Late at night when there was no one to call. No one to talk to. No one to walk me home.

I had this. I had it all.

As the chorus came, I raised the mic to the air. I thrust it out to the crowd and let a sea of people who would never really know me sing the words of my heart. My sequined dress swayed around me, and the plastic roses they had stuck into my braid poked my skull.

But I kept dancing. I kept swaying. I kept singing.

And I stood in my melodies alone. I spoke to the crowd only, and I said: "Hey Nashville. Who's ready to follow the music with me?"

TRACK 9
"FOREVER 18"

*written by Mia Peters in a collection
called* Missing Neverland

MIA

I'm encased by thorns as the last piece of her story wilts away. Flipping the pages, there's nothing left. The grave of the tin-can telephone sits empty, and this is it. After all this, she's standing alone on that stage. She lost the love, lost her home, lost it all except the dream that wasn't enough for her anymore.

"Mia . . ." Britt starts.

I shake my head, the pages crumple slightly, and that just makes me want to cry more because I ruin everything I touch, I . . . can't stop the sobs.

"This is *it*?" I wave the pages and Britt gently pulls them from my grasp, wrapping her arms around me. "Where's my dad? Where's her dream? Where's that surety?"

"Here." She places her hand over my heart, but her tone wavers. "There's got to be more. Maybe we didn't find all of it. There's no purpose to this being the end."

I cry into her shoulder, and it all comes out. There's no purpose to this ending. Tori Rose was taken too soon, she shined too bright, and every word on those last pages makes me think she really did wish she hadn't shot so high.

How is this it? After that last chapter where it seemed so clear she was desperate to have it all, how could she end up with nothing? How could she point me this way all this time just to sweep my revelations away with reality?

As Britt holds me, I wrap my arms around her too, trying to stay here. I try not to let it all spiral down and lose my breath and my heart and everything just like my mother did. When I can breathe again, Britt and I search the garden, the grounds, every envelope within my purse. There is nothing, nothing to fix this, nothing to show what she meant.

She did all this for me, and I ruined that too because I was so sure, so *convinced* I knew her message. I was so confident that I figured it out beneath the rose-tainted spotlight in the theater yesterday. Everything felt right with Britt, with Lost Girls, with the music, *everything*. But it felt right to Tori Rose too. Maybe dreams are always meant to fade, maybe we fall for their illusion and that's just what it is—an illusion, bright and bursting and never meant to be held.

The words blur again, the envelopes melt together before my eyes. And everything makes more or less sense as I stare at them lined up along the gravel path and note the pattern.

Regret You.

It's where her career led, where her music led, where her hunt for *me* led. Hell, even the poster one of the entries was hidden behind was from that album. The message couldn't have been clearer if it slapped me in the face.

"She . . ." I cover my mouth. I'm going to throw up. "I thought I knew. I thought I figured this out. I thought she was telling me to go and do this."

We've reached the front again, and we fall onto the porch

swing. Those initials she carved into it taunt me. *TR + DS were here.* What does she want me to get from that—from any of this?

I love Britt, I love the music, I love this band, but my mom is telling me that'll just make it harder when I inevitably lose them all.

I race to the railing, and everything inside of me comes out over those perfect pink roses.

"I don't think that's the ending." Britt shakes her head, holding back my hair as I heave. She rubs my back softly, close to tears herself. I hate that I make her cry with me; I hate that I make her hurt. I hate myself for every moment I've caused her pain and every grief-stricken spell I've ever cast across the people I love by being and looking like Tori Rose.

Maybe I was right all along and none of this changes that. Maybe it's good for her to lose me. Maybe she's better off that way. Maybe I'll just keep hurting her.

Britt continues. "When you think of the effort she had to put into this hunt, why would this be the ending she chose? Especially when . . ."

She doesn't have to finish. I know her well enough—and I know this town's favorite tragic tale of stardom well enough—to know what she was going to say. *Especially when this was the only ending she got to choose.*

"What if this was it, though?" My fingers dig into my arms as if I can wake myself up to a world where my mom is here and takes this back. Each inhale stabs, each exhale sets the tears loose again. "What if she's trying to show me everything she regrets? She was so eager to leave. What if she regrets it all? What if she regrets the journey?"

"Mia."

"What if she regrets Patrick and David or whoever my dad is?"

"Mia."

"What if she regrets the dream?"

"*Mia.*" Britt's voice cracks, and she wipes my tears with

her thumbs, kisses the spots they left their marks. "Please, Mia. Babe, just breathe."

I can't, I can't, I *can't*. "What if she regrets me?"

Britt's silence in response to this question tells me to look her way. "You're not your mom, Mia. You're not." It should be a relief, it should be an insult, I should *know* how to feel about that.

But my entire life, I've been shown how I am or am not her. My entire existence is a Venn diagram between me and Tori Rose. Maybe I got too much of the bad, too much of her tragedy, too much of the music's curse.

I thought I was finally finding the truth. Maybe I just had. I guess, if these clues say anything, maybe the truth just wasn't what I wanted to hear.

"What if that's us?" I whisper my fears as Britt rests her arm around my shoulders. I just want her to say we'll be okay. I just want her to promise that we won't fall apart. I've never been more scared to lose her, to lose everything—what's the difference?—to the open road. "What if we regret it too?"

Britt shakes her head. "Mia, I've seen you this week. I've seen you for years as you come into the music and refuse it. She doesn't own it. Her story doesn't own you."

"Neither of us know her. Not really."

"I know *you*."

"I don't know me." Sobs choke me again, and I'm so fucking lost.

I remember when Britt told me how the band decided on the name Lost Girls. "*To love the music is to never grow up, right?*" And I knew then and there that to love a girl was to know that you had to, sometimes without her.

I say, "I thought I'd finally decided who I am, but I don't know. I don't want to pick the wrong plan. Britt, what if this is the wrong plan?"

Another beat of silence passes.

Her words are too careful, too measured like my question sliced too deep. "Mia, just focus on this."

"I can't."

"I've told you I can't stay," Britt says. She scoots away from me—the distance between us is earthshaking, groundbreaking. Her eyes speak sorrows, but body language speaks distance. "I have to leave in two days. I'm not questioning the plan now."

"Why not?" I whisper for the first time. Why won't she save herself?

She doesn't meet my eyes—I've finally ruined this thing between us. I can tell from the curve of her lips and dimness in her gaze at the question. Last night we found each other, and now I've already lost us again. "You don't get to ask me that. Even if you're not, I'm sure about this, and your mom's ending doesn't change that. It doesn't have to change if you're sure either."

"I thought I was." My mother's absence hits harder than it ever has—because the goodbye I had before, which was nothing, was nowhere near as painful as this, and I didn't think that was possible.

"And now you're not?" Britt says.

"I don't know what to do. I'm sure about you, Britt. That won't change. But if she's trying to tell me—"

And I break her too. "Mia, I can't *do* this. I love you. I want you there, but I can't watch you hurt yourself like this. I'm done watching you be scared. Do you love the music?"

"Yes."

"Let's find the answers together," she says. "Let's not do this. Not again. Take a second and tell me what your dreams are saying to you, not what your mother is—*your own dreams.*"

The pause is heavier, and the weight comes back, threatens to crush me for good.

"My dreams don't speak to me," I lie, and her eyes call me on it, but her lips don't.

Britt's expression closes, too neutral and all guarded. "Then that's your first mistake." She starts to walk away.

"Britt, I'm sorry."

Britt shakes her head, walks backward along the drive, wiping furiously at her eyes. "Stop just saying that. If you're sorry for everything, what's the point? What's the point of this, any of it, if you refuse to do something and mean it? I know how much you want to know her, but you know her enough that you can't honestly tell me she'd want you to stay here and play it safe. All you do is play it safe."

"I . . ."

Britt takes another step back. "Mia. I can't *do* this. I'm not staying. I'm not questioning my dream. I'm not doing this." This time I know she's done with me, and the two goodbyes before me tangle together and hit me with the force of a riptide. She turns on her heel without another word.

"Britt, I'm so sorry." I stop right behind her on the sidewalk.

She pauses at her car, back to me, arms still crossed. "Do you need a ride home?"

"No, I need you," I say, and it aches harder when the words leave than when I hold them inside.

"I need to go," she says, and without looking at me again, she slips into her car. "I'll say goodbye now to make it easier for us both."

I stand there, on the cracked sidewalk beneath the summer sun and know this thing between us is finally mine to lose, and I did. She drives away, and I'm left with a crumpled, hopeless diary entry in my hand, envelopes and lyrics behind me, and nothing to show for it.

MIA

The inn doesn't shine, doesn't light my way home. The R in *Rose* is dimming, and in the loss of its light, the once-name of this place, *Peters*, is invisible.

Behind me, the door to our house slams and defeats any chance I have at slipping by unnoticed. Grams peeks out of her study—a small room home solely to her vintage desk and the fairytale picture books she writes and illustrates. At the end of the hall, Nana sits at the table, eating leftover pizza and watching *Gilmore Girls* on the living room television.

Both of them read my face at the exact same time, and it happens in slow motion and too fast. They get up in synchrony, rush toward me, crush me in the comfort of their embrace. Hugs like this from my grandmas have gotten me through nightmares, intangible grief, and one terrible school dance, but they've never had to get me through a broken heart in quite this way. I don't know if they can.

"I made my choice," I whisper. I'm a mess of breathless sobs and unfinished melodies that have lost all purpose. I am *exactly* like my mom for once. I lost it all, and I deserved to.

"That doesn't sound very convincing." Grams rocks from side to side.

"We love you," Nana says immediately with her usual confidence and forcefulness without knowing how I messed up the two things that mattered most. "No matter what."

At this point, I don't even know if I've earned that, not after how I've hurt Britt and Lost Girls and my mother. Their love is too good, too kind, the one thing unbroken by our story.

"What happened?" Grams says and pulls back a little, her dark brown eyes so open.

Nana's arm wraps fiercely around my shoulders, and they both guide me to the couch where they sit on either side of me like they did the other night.

I struggle to find the words—*any* words. I can't talk about Britt yet, not with the look on her face still seared behind my eyelids. So I speak to the other heartbreak in the room. "I failed Mom."

"No," Grams says at the same time Nana says, "Are you kidding?"

"She left me a hunt." I pull the journal out of my bag. "That's what led me to the guitar. I had to fill in the pieces, follow her trail. And I failed. Britt . . ." My tone trembles on her name. "We just finished it."

"You didn't fail her, Mia." Grams swallows hard. "There's so much of the good of her in you."

Not enough. There's too much of the other stuff. And I no longer know if that's something I should revel in. My mother took for granted the people in her life, and so did I. I'm as bad as this town, claiming I want the real her and ignoring her mistakes, *repeating* her mistakes.

But Grams keeps going. "She was a free spirit, full of wanderlust and nostalgia. All she ever wanted was to escape. I never completely understood what she was running from, but as

someone who had been running my whole life, I . . . I told her
to go. I didn't want her to ever be told she was too loud or too
much or living wrong, loving wrong." This last bit hits home,
and I see the way both of my grandmothers tense, the way they
reach for each other's hands and my own.

We've all been running.

"She left." Nana gives a hurt laugh. "I still wonder what
we did wrong that made her need to get away so desperately."

Grams squeezes her hand. "I don't think it was ever about
that."

And this is what I needed all those years, to grieve her with
them and not separately, to know something like they did.

"It wasn't about that," I tell them because they need to know.
I recall how she didn't call them, how the music distracted her,
but it was never for lack of love.

Everything that's happened this summer—save for my im-
ploding supernova of a relationship with Britt—comes tumbling
from my lips. I pull the seven envelopes from the book, and
my grandmothers look with me. Grams's eyes water as she flips
through them, and Nana's fingers clench her knees, knuckles
white and mouth agape while she takes it in. I tell them where
I've been, the destinations Britt and I reached and the things I
discovered about her—the people I met.

"How . . ." Nana trails off, for once speechless. "I don't . . ."

I hug my arms to my stomach. "The whole hunt wound
up at her album *Regret You*. She was clearly showing me that
she regretted leaving and meeting my father and . . . She clearly
regretted me. Everything that led *her* to me was in this diary."

The silence is thick once again. I'm left suffocated, waiting
for the release of noise.

"Your mother loved you very much, Mia." Grams says. Once
again, she starts from the beginning and she guides us through

a tale. When I was younger, we'd read exactly three books each night before bed, many of them her own. I can hear nursery rhymes in her voice like I can hear lyrics in my mother's. "She came home while she was pregnant with you and, oh my, that girl had always hated studying and planning and following the rules. But for you, she did it all. She read every book she could get her hands on, wiped the parenting section of the Cove Bookstore clean. She painted the nursery herself. Your room is still the rose gold she chose. She was so scared. I'd never seen her that way. She was worried she was going to mess this up. I told her there wasn't a chance in hell, and look at you now. Our brave, beautiful girl. You are everything she had hoped you'd be. You are."

I don't know how to believe those words in the memory of my actions and the bleak ending to the story she penned for me.

"I thought I was going to leave," I admit. "When you told me to decide, that's what I decided. That's what I thought she wanted."

"What do you want?" Nana says.

I shrug. "I don't know." *Liar.* "I was terrified I'd regret everything. That I'd lose myself and . . . and Britt, if we ever found the spotlight. I'm scared to leave the only town that's ever shown me a piece of my mom. The place she was buried. Where I grew up. This house. I'm scared, and I don't want to be a coward."

"Then don't be," Grams says, like it's that simple.

It would've been easier if their answer had been *stay.* Then I'd fall back into life as it was, let Britt go, let this go. I'd have to.

"How do you find the rest of her story?" Grams asks, and there's something there, something that says there's more.

"I need to talk to my dad," I say before I can stop myself. That wasn't in the clues, wasn't in the answer, but I need someone who knows her in a different way, who saw things on the road that even they didn't.

They both freeze.

"Why?" Nana asks.

"I need to know his side of the story." I shift, bookended by them.

"His side is leaving you." The angles of Nana's features have never looked more severe.

Grams squeezes my hand once more. "You're vulnerable right now."

"You said you wanted me to know her."

"*Her.*" Nana shakes her head. "Please, Mia. Let's leave it at that."

They're still hiding him.

I retract my grip, slide off the couch, and stand, hoping they'll see I'm not a little girl anymore, even if I still make a mess of things.

"I need to know," I say. Grams asked me how to find the rest of her story, and that's the only thing I have right now, the only thing I can control.

Except I can't.

"No," Nana says. "You're not talking to him."

"I'm eighteen years old."

"You're under this roof."

All the pent-up pain releases. "Then you lied too." I regret it instantly.

"Manners," Grams snaps.

They sit on our old brown sofa with Stars Hollow paused on the television behind me and the window overlooking the forest of Sunset Cove to my side.

I stare, plead with my eyes, but they don't bend.

Scooping up the story, I walk away. I shove my guilt aside because there's too much of it right now. I slam my bedroom door behind me and I flop on my bed, but all I can think of is last night, that perfect night, as I stare at glow-in-the-dark stars on the opposite wall, around the mirror.

I study the way my hair falls to my collarbone, sandy blond. My eyes are blue. My T-shirt slips off my shoulder, and I look for those pieces of Tori Rose that have people recognizing me—not sure if I'm hoping to find her or miss her in my own features.

I remember every time I've held her album covers next to my face in the mirror.

Today, there are too many similarities, too many differences, too much of everything. I grab a facial wipe from my makeup bag and I scrub it all off—eyeliner, eye shadow, lipstick, blush, foundation. I don't relent until I'm clean.

When I'm done, what's left is just me, and I can't look in the mirror any longer.

MIA

Sitting at the counter of the Horizon, the whole place looks different—whether that be because of the girl I always came here with or witnessing the continuous excitement over the karaoke machine. People use it without end, enjoying the music. It all pulls me back into the diary, makes me wonder what it would've been like to see her sing—to sing with her here.

Whether or not I'd want to.

Linnea's eyes are clouding again, and I place my hand over hers, having finished my shift. I still haven't quite processed the fact that Britt no longer works here. *Because she leaves in two days.*

How is it still the same day as when we slipped out at sunrise to go to that house? It's only been hours since Miner Lane and since my argument with my grandmas. Time stretches into small pockets of eternity, at least for now. Soon, she'll move on, she'll move away, and I'll be here.

She'll be okay. At this point, the only thing I want is for her to be okay.

"It's so weird to watch this again." Linnea smiles through her tears. "I know I saw Lost Girls using it, but seeing everyone like this . . . She owned that stage, you know. Her initials were scratched into it with a penny. The top right corner. Her own doing, of course."

"I know."

Linnea gazes at me softly. "Sing something. Take a turn."

"Linnea, I can't." I can't go on that stage and act like everything is fine. I can't touch a foot to that surface without picturing Britt, hearing the lyrical cadence of her voice, remembering the words she'd whisper beneath the canopy of midnight.

More than that, I can't go on that stage without remembering my mother, without becoming her.

Linnea gives me a look. "A little bird told me you sang at Back to Me & You the other night. Won't you sing for me?"

And I don't know how to say no to that.

When the latest couple—two girls with vividly dyed hair, crop tops, and fraying denim skirts—gets down from the stage, I walk across the room and up those steps. Taking a deep breath, I catch sight of the initials from the lighthouse, from the porch swing, and from here.

TR was here.

She regretted it; she regretted this; she regretted me.

Yet here I am.

Stepping up to the karaoke machine, I fiddle around and find the track I'm looking for—"Don't Stop Believin'," like Lost Girls chose, like Patrick Rose and my mom did. I don't know why I do it, but I pick up the mic, click play. I begin to sing, and I hate how momentarily the tension releases.

Linnea's hands clap over her mouth, and she watches me as the tears collecting in her eyes begin to fall. I sing it to her and the stained-glass portrait of the sunset over the door, the door every person in this town has walked through whether it be for the music, the food, or the company.

It was supposed to heal a bit of the confusion, make me feel closer to her in a way that meant something again. But it only leaves me thinking about other small-town girls and midnight trains leading anywhere and everywhere.

As the song ends, my attention falls on someone else, drumming their fingers against the mosaic surface of a table, casting quick glances my way. Someone else I hurt. Setting the mic down atop the machine, I study his face. I hop down from the stage and let the next group—drunk college frat guys from SCCC—take over as I walk toward that table and that boy.

Sitting there, staring at me, is Jess with a group of friends. Jess whose window I climbed out of just to avoid any conflict, feelings, or confrontation.

He turns away the moment he sees me coming.

"Hey." I tap his shoulder.

He stiffens immediately, but with slow, lazy motions, he tries to look like he couldn't care less even though his eyes speak the other story—they always do.

"Can I talk to you?" I ask.

Jess glances at his usual gang—a group of three guys and two girls from our grad group. One of the guys wolf whistles and I ignore him.

"Now?" Jess says, and there's a slight edge to his voice.

"Yes. Please."

Casting one last glance at his friends, he gets to his feet reluctantly, and I lead him to the opposite end of the counter from where Linnea's busying herself—still visibly weepy from my song.

"What's up, Mia?"

"I probably shouldn't have climbed off your roof," I say.

"You think?"

"Look, I'm . . . I'm sorry, Jess." I say it. I mean it. I'm sorry for running, for leaving, for always being so scared. I try to put that all into those three words.

I'm sorry, Jess.

He leans back. "It's all right."

What?

Everything I planned to say falls away, and I stare at him, looking up to meet his eyes. "What?"

He still frowns, but he says, "Gave me a good story for college, my ex-girlfriend jumping out my bedroom window, and I guess I knew you were in love with someone else. I just thought for a minute . . ." He shakes his head.

His penetrating stare and the ease with which he says those words floor me.

"How's Britt?" he asks, and that's the icing on the cake I burned.

"I wouldn't know," I say, and I drop my gaze.

He studies me for a few seconds, and it's too long, and I think I might regret everything that led up to this but, somehow, I still don't regret *this* moment and this apology. Maybe even if everything else is twisted and wrong, that's a bit of progress on its own.

Jess gives me a pointed look. "Maybe you should look back sometimes when you're running away. And think about why you're really leaving."

This time, he's the one to walk away.

Outside Britt's house, the moon shines brighter, illuminating the driveway where we've kissed beneath the streetlights. I stand at the bottom of it, gaze stuck on the trunk of her car and the boxes piled so high they block the window. They're a reminder of what I already know; she's leaving Sunset Cove, with or without me. And, at this rate, I may never see her again.

I think of what Jess said and I don't know exactly how I wound up here, but I need to apologize before she leaves. I need to tell her those words she deserves to hear.

I don't know why I run, what I'm running from, but I ran *somewhere* at least. Here.

Walking slowly up the slope of the driveway, I'm about to step up the one stair to the door when it opens and Britt walks out with another box—this one full of the records she collects.

She's shifting it in her arms, wearing another Taylor Swift T-shirt. Her eyes widen at the sight of me here, and as I open my mouth to say something, she walks right by me without a word.

I stand behind her. "Britt . . ."

"Mia." She opens the side door of her car and shoves the box in, slamming it closed and whipping around to face me. "What are you doing here? Figure yourself out?"

"I'm so sorry," I say.

"I need you to go." She looks away.

"Britt, I . . ."

She shakes her head.

"I'm—"

"Go. *Please.*"

There's a long pause in which both of us drop our gazes, and then I go, because she's telling me to and I have to listen and accept this heartbreak I earned. As I step away, our paths cross again in what feels like slow motion—her heading in and me heading out. She turns her cheek, and her front door shuts, and all I hear in its closing is the echo of dead dreams.

MIA

I don't go home. From Britt's house, I bike off, the rose charm on my handlebars tapping against the grips with each push forward. The streets are silent this late, and the countdown is almost down to one day. This is almost tomorrow's problem, her leaving.

My hair flies out of its loose ponytail, and my denim jacket is caught in the wind, but I keep going, one destination on my mind. Past verandas and beach houses and this town I call home.

It takes half an hour, it takes all my breath, but I wind up along the sandy shore at Britt and my cove. Guiding my bike the rest of the way in a walk, I slip between the rock faces and inhale the salt of the sea.

Sitting on the cold, wet ground, I tug off my shoes, toss them aside. They hit the rock and land in a pile as I slip into the ocean. I let the water consume me, overwhelm me, become me. With each backstroke I imagine these shallow waves absorbing all this and bringing it back to the sea, into something vaster and greater than me.

Just yesterday with Britt is under the surface every time I dive, every time I close my eyes to keep the sting out of them. And yesterday morphs into last year which morphs into the year before in a whirlwind of what we had. The memories are too much, too many, and I surface to a faint ping from my phone. For one foolish second, I wish on every star it's Britt, summoned by the reminiscence, saying to come back, saying to come talk. It's not.

It's a notification from Instagram:

"Direct Message from @thesaraellis"

She actually . . .

Fingers pruned and frantic, shaking so hard my touch ID can't unlock it, I open Instagram. Britt's latest picture is at the top of my feed. It's from this afternoon with her and Amy and Sophie standing in front of her car. The caption says *summer lovin'*.

I click on my inbox instead, and there it is, a message from Sara Ellis—the pianist of Fate's Travelers, now a solo artist with more followers than the other still-living members of the band combined. She actually replied.

Today, 7:39 p.m.

@thesaraellis: Mia. Wow, I haven't heard that name in a while. You know, Tori was visiting my tour when she decided on it? She was sitting in my dressing room, doing my makeup and chatting about your town, talking about this woman she wanted to name you for. She was seven months pregnant, waddling around, and she insisted on driving up to see my show. Your dad was out of town, so Mateo and Edie went down to get her (Edie and I lived together for a while before M proposed to me, and she and Tori moved in together).

I love that she left you a hunt. I still remember the day she died. The world lost a light that day. She was music, fully and completely. We respected, admired, and supported each other, and you know what? For all the pain her passing caused, I am so glad I met her, that she was part of my life. That's the funny thing about loss, you know? You wish you'd never had to feel a hurt that deep, but you *knew* that person and you wouldn't have had it any other way. For however long they were there, they meant something, and that is forever. That's what that word means. At least in my experience. I'm sure your grandmothers feel the same. I wrote a song about it. It's dedicated to her: Field of Roses, if you ever want to hear another story from her friend.

As far as the music goes, I can't help you there. It's such an individualized experience. I know I was scared out of my mind the first day I drove up to Music City. I was still scared when Fate's Travelers took off. I was the first to leave the band, and that may have been the most terrifying moment of my life, but I'm glad I was part of it. I'm glad I knew them too. And I'm glad I left. Your mother was the picture-perfect country star that the music world wanted, and I grew tired of working twice as hard to be seen in a band I started. So I set out on my own, because I was young and passionate and aching to be heard for me. I loved Edie, your mother, and Mateo, and I loved the music. It was time for it to become mine again. I needed some space to take that back. Mateo found me again first, of course. Tori and I drifted in and out of each other's circles and then crashed together once more. And escaping Edie was like escaping quicksand. That girl slept on my couch for a solid year between gigs.

Long story short, I found my music. Your mother found hers. Is yours worth chasing? You're the only one who can decide that. She can pave the path, but she can't guide you down it. I can tell you this, but I can't tell you what to do. I know she's gone, but her story isn't over. She didn't end the day she died.

And I can tell you, for the record, that the Tori Rose I knew never did linger long in regrets. Did she have them? Sure. We all do. Did I? Yes. But not about the music. Did Patrick? Edie? Mateo? Absolutely. So fucking many. But never about each other. And Tori's regrets? Trust me, they were never about you.

xo Sara

My heart skips a beat as I read the last words of her message. I pull myself onto the rock and sink down. She says her story isn't over, she says she didn't regret me. How does this make sense with how the hunt ended?

Unless the hunt isn't over. Unless there's more to find.

Dazed and searching for the perfect response, I pull up the song Sara wrote on YouTube, greeted by its thirty-seven million views. There's no music video. The backdrop is of pink roses, and there are no lyrics, just windchimes and humming and the piano, strong and melancholic, hopeful in all the hopelessness, quieting where you'd expect her to crescendo and vice versa. Everything unexpected.

As the evening air nips my cheeks, I play it again.

I scroll down to the comments.

RIP a legend

She will be missed

Beautiful, Sara.

</3 goodbye

These people missed her, these people saw her. And Sara's tribute carried that on for these seven minutes before they forever split ways. Maybe everyone remembers her differently, maybe her story continues every time she's remembered past her death. Maybe, in that way, her life never truly ended.

I stumble over to where my shoes landed, humming along to the tune. And when I lean down to pick them up, water slips from my collarbone to the ground, landing on a set of initials that in all my times here I'd never looked for, never seen.

TR was here.

MIA

I'm alone in the quiet lot with "Don't Stop Believin'" and "Field of Roses" as I return to our house by the inn. Keeping as silent as possible, I inch inside and across the hardwood floor, sliding my shoes off and avoiding any floorboard that whines.

"Mia," Nana says the second I cross the threshold to the kitchen. "You're home."

She and Grams sit at the table, each holding a mug of hot chocolate while they watch me.

I stop. "I just went to the Horizon for a bit. Then I needed to clear my head. I sang a song." They both ignore my damp clothes.

"We know." Grams smiles at me in a way she never has because of the music. "Linnea called us."

"Oh."

"Come sit."

I do as they say. I sit in the spot I've had since I was a little girl, right beside where my mom once scratched her initials into the table. I take in our mismatched home and the pictures on the walls.

"Mia," Grams starts. "Things got a little out of hand this morning."

I hold back my apologies, because even though I regret the way I spoke, I still don't regret the things I said. I deserve my history, my past, my story, and seeing as it connects to my mother's, I should not be the one kept in the dark. I want to believe her story isn't over, but I can't unless I see all the pieces.

"We want you to know we're always here for you," Grams adds. "It's just . . . your father was distant. He and your mom were a turbulent match at best, and he left you so soon after your mom . . . passed. We didn't want you to have to deal with that."

I begin to speak, but Grams holds up a finger, telling me it's not my turn. "But now we see you finding her story and drafting your own. You *are* a bold, brave young lady, and it's so hard to realize you're all grown up and not still that baby girl, but we love you more every day." She must see the tears in my eyes along with the denial because she adds, "That love is independent from whatever mistakes you make. We will always love your mother. We will always love you. Wherever you are. Whoever you are. Whatever you do."

I clench the arms of the chair and drop my gaze as the last confessions spill out in their openness and trust. "The only person I would've left with won't talk to me. What's worse is I don't blame her. At all. It's like I need people, I need someone with me, like it'll make me whole again or whatever, but I leave them because I'm scared they'll leave first. I'm scared, and she was the only one who made me feel brave."

"Only you can fix that," Nana says, echoing the words from Sara's message that gave me another little part, another view of my mom. Hearing my grandmas say it, I wish I was still little and they could bandage all my scrapes, kiss all my scars better, make my problems go away. But I'm not and they can't. "The people who love you will be with you even when they're gone. You deserve that. You deserve that timeless love. Even when you fuck up." I laugh at her language, just a little. Nana adds, "Even when you think you're too much. We have one thing we can fix now, though."

I look back and forth between them.

Grams leans forward and hands me a slip of paper, folded carefully and written across in her usual neat handwriting—so different from her daughter's carefree scrawl. I slide it open, and it's a phone number.

It's a phone number.

It's . . .

"Go call him," Grams says.

The phone sits on my bed—about to reveal who my father is, who my country star mother settled down with for a while. That number waits for me, and the part of me that *needs* her, needs the truth, wants this too. It's something I can have even if I don't let myself follow my songs. It's another thing to hold on to that, even if everyone leaves, will always be mine.

My story, hopelessly intertwined with hers.

When I can't take the silence a second longer, I step closer. Hands shaking a little less than before, I picture that stage, and that song returns to me. Journey takes me to where she started her voyage. I felt it in that second, suspended in time, when I sang it for Linnea—for Patrick Rose and my mother and David Summers.

I felt her beginning before mine ever got its chance.

Each number I dial is a promise, and I follow it through, press the phone to my ear.

"Hello?" I exhale too quickly as I hear his voice for the first time, which is somewhere between high and low, gravelly and smooth, assured and quiet. The television drones in the background, and a woman's laughter rings out nearby.

"Hi," I say. "My name's Mia Peters . . . In case you forgot, I'm your daughter."

The quiet that falls over the line is both fulfilling and deafening, and I've wanted to say this to my absentee father who left me without a word for so long.

I listen to his breathing, but he seems to have stopped. There's a shuffling, a muttering, and then the background noise fades and a door shuts.

"Mia," he says like he's testing my name, the way Edie did when she opened up to me. "It's good to hear from you."

"It would've been nice to hear from you."

"How did you get this number?" The words become wary and guarded. He doesn't apologize for leaving, ask me how I've been, tell me he misses me. I don't know how he would—how he'd miss someone he doesn't know—but I missed my mother every day even before I knew her story.

"My grandmas gave it to me. I need to talk to you."

Another silence until he says, "I owe you so many apologies."

There's a sick satisfaction in hearing him say that.

I settle in for this talk, but my bed doesn't feel like a safe place to sit. Nowhere in this room is left untouched by Britt's memories, so I claim the floor, and I pull my knees to my chest.

"I'm sorry," my father says. "I shouldn't have left you. I should've called, but time went on—"

"That's what time tends to do."

"You already remind me of her." When he says it, it feels different than the times I've been told that before.

"I don't know how I should feel about that."

"Your mother was brilliant, so I'd reckon pretty damn good."

"Tell me about her," I say.

"Um, well." He clears his throat, and I try to picture him, face ever-shifting. "I think she was my soulmate, in every way but one."

"What way was that?" I'm leaning forward like we're talking across a kitchen table, like this is a casual conversation not a life-changing one.

"She was in love with someone else."

My heart hammers, and the words build, and I know they're going to make their way into this moment, but I have to pick and choose which ones survive. I need him to keep talking. "Are you . . . is your name Patrick Rose?"

Nothing.

Finally, he says, "Yes. I see your grandmas really did hide me. Just like your mom did."

"What do you mean my mom hid you?" My father is Patrick Rose. I am Patrick and Tori Rose's daughter, Mia Emily Peters. The child of the lead singers of Fate's Travelers.

Her daughter and . . . his.

My mother didn't pick David, didn't pick love, but she wasn't all alone either. What did that mean? This is the in-between, the missing pages.

They were all right. Her story isn't over.

He sighs. "Tori loved to keep moving, but the constant attention got the best of her. She wanted our relationship to stay a secret. She was never really the same when she and her best friend stopped talking, but she was still all the best of life. The chaos. The fun. The joy. It was just forced now, artificial zest in the place of a once-careless girl. She sang songs, wrote records, she was everything she ever wanted to be and none of what she planned. She didn't want to get married, half the time didn't want me, but I stuck around for a while. And then longer . . . when I found out about you. This town kept me like it'd always trapped her, without even realizing who I was. It really is where the sun sets on dreams."

That shouldn't piss me off and fuck me up and hurt me so deeply at once. I don't want the sun to set on the life I was living this week before I gave up on it. I don't want the sun to set on me like it did on them.

He stayed . . . when he found out about me. Was I what ended his dream?

"What happened to you? Did you keep singing?" I want to know more. I want to know where he is along the coast, who that woman he's moved on with is, where he is now.

Another sigh escapes him. "For small-town weddings and sometimes as a special guest on your mom's tours. I wasn't really the star I thought I was. I realized that before our band broke up. I wasn't like her."

"Then why did you leave?" *Why did you leave me too when you were the parent who didn't have to?*

"Your mom and I had problems, Mia. We were fire and fire, and then we were ice and ice. We were always on the same page and never on the same side. We took long breaks, we messed it up all the time and never fell back in sync. She told me we were done for good before she went on her last tour, and she never came back from it, and the guilt I felt that our last goodbye was the way it was . . . I can't explain it. So I ran away. I'm sorry."

"Sorry doesn't change anything."

"You're pretty jaded, aren't you?"

"You don't get to say that." When he doesn't reply to that, I take a shot. "Did she regret it?" I heard it from Sara, I heard it from my grandmothers, but I need it from him too, I need the word of the man she chose. Especially if I was what made them stay together . . . if I was unexpected.

"What?"

"The dream? The songs?" My voice cracks. "Me?"

He sucks in a breath, and it almost sounds like it hurts him too. "No. Neither of us did."

My chest loosens, my next breath comes easier than the last.

But if she didn't regret it, why did she dedicate an album to that intention? If he didn't regret it, how could he disappear from the spotlight and my life?

"Did she regret anything?" I ask. Sara spoke of them all having regrets.

He laughs. "If she did, only tequila and nightclubs know. I . . . probably shouldn't have told you that."

"Stories are better than your silence." I look around my room, and I grab my purse. I spread the envelopes across my window seat, one at a time. I set the pages those letters led to in bundles behind them, smoothing creases, letting the stories sit. "How did you end up together?"

"We didn't see each other for a while after our band broke up, but I kept thinking of her. I kept hearing her songs. I went back to Sunset Cove just to see and turns out she was visiting. She was there. At the inn. In front of the piano again. We called it destiny."

"Are you still in Sunset Cove?"

"No."

"Will you tell me where you are?" Again, his feed on Instagram comes to mind, ocean waves and sandy beaches.

Another pause rattles the room, and then he shows how little he's really sorry, how much he truly regrets: "Not yet. After a while, I wanted to hide too."

"Maybe this wasn't about you."

"Tell me about you then."

I shake my head, and he can't see that because he's not here. This departure was the only one I *didn't* deserve. "You don't get my story yet. But when you're ready to see me or call me or try to be here . . . maybe I'll give you a piece of it."

"Mia, I'm sorry," he says again.

I stare at those envelopes and the sky out my window, and I hang up the phone.

Around four in the morning, I'm still sitting before my window seat after copious amounts of ice cream and *Gilmore Girls* with my grandmas. Britt officially leaves in one day.

I can't sleep, tossing and turning, new lyrics spinning to life in my mind, making it impossible to tune out everything I found and said goodbye to so fast. The rainbow of letters stares back at me, unrelenting, and something prickles at the back of my mind—a missing detail. Like when I couldn't place where I knew Edie, where her features lined up in my manufactured memory from Google interviews and concert videos.

Something is missing.

Sara and Patrick's stories were between the last and second-to-last pages, something clearly happened in that time. That's where the real answer lies, and I don't know my mom fully, I never met her at an age I can recall, but after everything, she can't have left me like this. Britt was right about that, about all of it.

The last message—the cryptic nature of it—makes me stumble more than once, and no matter how many times I sit here and read and imagine texting Britt or climbing through her window and seeing her, I keep coming back to it. Fingers flying across the pages, the letters, the lyrics, I rearrange them.

It's drifting off, head on the edge of the bench and hair scattered around her spread-out story, that the words click together.

Each track in an album has a number to correspond with the song, the array of colors in a rainbow have an order, and my mom said she wished she was always only a call away, but she's never been a call away, so . . .

The clue was found in a tin can telephone. If I order the envelopes from red to purple and write the numbers of the songs in their respective albums . . .

I pull a basket of my mother's CDs out from my closet, grab a pen and Post-it notes from my desk, and I set to work. I don't know what propels it, what millisecond unraveled it, but when I'm done the entire hunt forms something new.

If I'm right, that was not my mother's last message in those diary pages. If I'm right, hidden in these letters, she's left me a phone number.

MIA

I dial new numbers into my phone, along with the Sunset Cove area code, and I click *call*.

Even waiting for my father to pick up, hearing him speak of a life before and after and with her and before and after and without me, I didn't feel this on edge. This is the last chance, the last-ditch effort to find the ending of her story, and in turn, a new start for my own.

"Please, Mom," I whisper.

The ringing is endless and intoxicating and my heart beats in time with it.

The phone finally goes to voicemail.

There's silence for a second, and I plummet. About to hang up, I do what I always do, and I fight the feelings because that is the only way I will get through them.

Then it starts. "Hi, Mia." The automated message takes my breath away. "Hi, love. It's your mom." My sob catches in my throat, just like when I uncovered her diary.

How did she *do* this?

She continues, and I hold on for every second that she speaks. Her voice is a little rougher than I would have expected. Still, the edge is cotton-soft, sunshine-warm, like in her interviews—like I always imagined it would be when she spoke to me.

"I debated this step of the hunt for a while," she says. "I'm so glad you figured it out. Thanks for taking this journey with me. We have three important things to cover before my time runs out. Unfortunately, my love, I'm going to have to be brief.

"First, I want you to know I love you, since you won't remember hearing it from me. I loved you the moment I saw you. You came out so quietly. I was a screamer myself. But you were this sweet, precious baby in my arms. So content to just be and exist. But make sure you live. Chase your dreams, sweetheart.

"I know the diary ended a little sad, but I wanted to tell you in person, in case words didn't translate. I will never regret chasing my dream. I regret the people I hurt. I regret the bridges I burned. I regret losing who I was in an attempt to find someone else in everyone else and within me. I created someone new entirely. Just to avoid mediocrity. But there is magic in all of it, and if you can hold on to the magic of the moment while chasing whatever your dreams are, you'll wind up so much better off than me. The smallest moments make the best music. Don't lose your people. I let down my moms, my friends, the love of my life, but it was not because of my music, it was because I was so set on losing sight of myself, on getting out.

"Second, I need you to deliver a letter. I know you're probably tired of my letters by now. Just this one. Please. There's someone I'd like you to talk to. You'll find it in my old desk in my old bedroom. If I know my moms, and I think I do, they've kept that thing. There's a compartment under the surface with a small latch. It blends in, but you should be able to find it if you look, if you've made it this far. Forgive the mess.

"Third, I swear I never made lists before I made this hunt. But I thought a lot when I found out I would have to say goodbye about this concept that was dear to me. As someone who spent my life singing, it hit me that I would have a last song in a way it never did before. I would have a last love song. I'd spent my life writing love songs. For everyone who caught my eye. Two boys in particular, as you know. Then one especially. But I never loved them the way I love you. I never loved anything or anyone the way I love you. Not even the music. That love is something I could not drive away. I cannot replace. I cannot pretend to forget. I love you wholeheartedly, and you are the one thing I never had to learn to regret any piece of.

"So here's my last love song. Here's my song for you."

The tears are steady as they carve paths down my features, and she begins to sing a song that never hit the radio. She sings a song, in this room, meant only for me.

I spent my life chasing fireflies, little lit-up dreams,
Floating lanterns and lost time, set on who I'm gonna be,
I collected promises and hearts and melodies on my sleeve,
I sang everything and anything, lost in the star I had to be.
I floated bottles out to sea with wishes to the sky,
Hoping the music inside me would forever be my guide,
The lighthouse roved the sea, but I was the one it
*   couldn't bring home,*
My wild heart was something no one could tame all on
*   their own.*
But then a song came from the silence, a glowing beacon
*   in my pain,*
A sunlit morning on the sidewalk, no one else catches
*   rainbows in the rain,*

And the regrets in my back pocket fell through the hole
  in my blue jeans,
I wouldn't give the world for what you mean to me.
I wouldn't trade secrets or erase mistakes for the love I
  have for you,
I'll never know another song, never hear a tune this
  true,
You plucked the thorns from roses and you put the sun
  back in the sky,
You were better than all the chasing, I loved you deeper
  in my disguise,
And, pursued by the waning limelight, I knew one thing
  that's for sure,
My last love song was not a thing for them, it was for
  you my baby girl.

There is no break in the tears, in the love I have for this woman who I will never meet, never hug, never be able to tell how much she means to me, but who I will always love even when I am old and gray and the spotlight has forever lost its allure.

I have never believed anything as much as I believe her in this moment—as much as I believe *in* her in this moment. All the fear dissipates at her voice, at this message, at these answers until it is just me and her, and I *believe* her.

She loves me. She doesn't regret me.

Everyone gets a last love song, a last chance to give their heart to the world. They don't always know when or how or where or with who it will go down. But my mother—my bold, brave, inspiring, hurricane of a mother who I'm finally learning real things about and meeting for the first time—she knew all of these things exactly. And here, on this machine, she chose to give her last love song to me.

"Please leave a message after the beep."

There is no escape from these feelings. For the very first time, I welcome them, I accept them, I accept this piece of me as something good, and her songs meet my own.

Beep.

MIA

Streams of people are leaving and the club is closing down when I rush inside Back to Me & You to find Edie.

I have to fix everything. I realized in the silence after that beep that I don't just want this dream because Tori Rose approves and told me to chase it. I wanted permission, a sign, but I also want to be able to own my last love song when it's time. I want to have an adventure like hers, a life that was felt and loved and lived. I want to be able to share my story one day and stand behind it.

I have one day to make it right.

At the other end of the club bathed in sunrise, Edie wipes wine stains off the large bar and ties up her pale purple hair. She said one last thing that night I sang, right before I left: "*Kid, please, when you find it, tell me why she did this. Tell me what she had to say.*"

"Hey, stranger," she says now. "How's your hunt?"

"I finished," I say. "I found the last piece of her story. It was a song. For me."

Edie stops wiping the counter, and under the dim signs

that swing their shadows across the bar, she looks older than I remember, like the grief aged her quicker than the music.

"Can I hear it?" she whispers.

I nod, planning to share it with my grandmas the second they wake up so that they can say goodbye too.

"Gwen, cash out for me?" Edie yells to the woman who's behind the counter with her. She's following me before she can respond. "Let's go."

Walking out the front and around the side of Back to Me & You, she unlocks that fifth door, and we step into my mother's past. Here, it's safe to dial those numbers and cry freely and listen to it again. This is my new favorite soundtrack and the first one of hers to tear me apart in this exact way. Edie hears it with me this time, tearing up with the first note of her voice, following it to the end—to the beep.

"She . . ." Edie covers her mouth with her hand, and she does the only thing that could surprise me at this point. She hugs me. "Thank you."

I hug her quickly, and we both shuffle away at the same time, wiping our eyes.

"Thank you for helping me," I say. "Thanks for caring about this journey."

"Come visit me before you go," Edie says. "I have more stories to share. So many. Oh, she was so much trouble. I loved her so damn much."

I don't know how Edie knows I want to leave, but there's a comfort in the fact that I don't have to hide it. No matter whether or not Britt will hear me out, I need to see something that's not preserved in my mother's name. I need to take her legacy and find more of this story that's turning into my own.

"I will. I can't wait to hear them . . . Do you have time for one now?"

Edie smiles the wicked smile from her band posters. "Sure thing. She's remembered for her voice and her mistakes. There was this one interview where a man had the nerve to ask her about her dating life and how he caught word she was quite the heartbreaker with all sorts of sleazy innuendos. She flashed a smile, looked at his wedding ring, and asked if he was sad he missed out on her wild days. She made so many mistakes, and she hurt people, and she lived and she breathed and she was human, and it took her years after our band disbanded to really own that, but once she did, she got her magic back. She found it again. We make so many fucking mistakes, Mia. She made so many. But don't know her by her mistakes. That's not all she was . . . that's not all you are. We are not a product of our mistakes. We're the sum of what we learn from them."

Her words end, and I hold on to them.

"Why did it end? The band?"

Edie just shrugs. "We outgrew each other. It happens. You can outgrow places and people and still love them. I know I do."

No one's ever said it like that to me before. I can outgrow Sunset Cove and still love it, still visit, see something else without the guilt.

"Hello?" Someone raps on the door we propped open with an abandoned beer case once again. A red-haired woman stands there.

Edie looks up and grins. "Hey, wife." Her eyes are so happy, gaze so fond, and it makes me think—along with her words—that maybe I deserve that happiness too.

"Hey, wife." The lady pokes her back, and she turns to me. Her eyes widen. "Jill Thorsted," she says, and she extends a hand which I shake. "You're Tori Rose's girl I take it?"

And this time, when that's how I'm recognized, I'm sure there is no one I'd rather be.

MIA

PRESENT DAY

From Back to Me & You, I head straight to where the letter my mom asked me to deliver leads—past the heartbreaks of Miner Lane, the cove, the sea, and right through the front door of the Sunrise Theater. I already know who I'm going to find, who I didn't recognize him as all those years or when I was here with Britt.

He's not standing behind the desk, but I have this feeling brought by a little bit of the fate my mother so purposefully believed in as to where he is. Walking past those posters, and back down the hall, I approach theater 3A, the site of his last show, the site of the rose spotlight.

"Hello?" I say.

There's a bang and someone says, "Ouch."

In the back, from beneath the tech booth, a man stands.

"David Summers?" I say, and he studies me in this nervous, aloof way.

He waves at me through the window, acknowledging this is

him, beckoning me to walk through the open door. He wipes his hands on a rag, tools thrown across the worktable and soundboard.

"What do you want?" he asks, and he's not the daring boy from the pages of my mother's diary.

"I'm—"

"Mia Rose," he says, stiffly. "Yeah, I know."

"Mia Peters, actually." I hold out a hand to him. "My mother's daughter, if I'm lucky."

He almost smiles. "How's your dad like that?" He busies himself rearranging a jar of pens and pencils with silly eraser toppers.

"I wouldn't know. He ran off before my first birthday," I say. This is David Summers, and my mother was in love with him, and even after my dad left for something more, he's still here in their town.

David shakes his head. "I'm sorry."

I hold out the letter with its loopy address and his name scrawled across the front with a heart. "I have a letter for you."

"I have a mailbox, you know."

"It's kind of a special delivery."

He sighs and finally faces me and really looks at me with weary green eyes as though this action takes everything out of him. "Fine. Let's see."

Handing it to him, I know he recognizes the writing on the front immediately from the way his jaw drops.

I didn't read the contents, but there's a new narrative in his features as he unfolds the pink stationery and reads it. His gaze is hard at first, cold and hurting in a way I know, in a way I liked to fake for the mirror and am trying to unlearn. As his eyes reach the second half of the first page—there are four pages, by the looks of it, with the back and front scrawled across—they begin to soften, and then they cloud by the middle of page two. His first tear falls, and I feel like

I'm intruding by the third, so I turn my cheek, watch the stage, no longer painted red.

He finishes with a crinkle of the paper as he refolds it, and he leans down and braces his hands on his worktable as he breaks down. "I miss her so much," he tells me.

"She loved you," I whisper, and it's so hard to say—those words can hurt so bad when you can't say them back.

"I know. I loved her. I still love her. So much." He doesn't hold back. "I should have told her when I had the chance."

"Did she . . . did she tell you?" That wasn't in the pages. It wasn't in her voicemail.

David swallows sharply, and he nods. "When we . . . parted ways, we wanted different things. We were in Nashville and I needed to go home, but she wanted me to stay. She told me she loved me, she wanted me, but she wanted the music more. You know, she came back one time? To see *Grease*. I saw her in the audience, and I couldn't even bring myself to say hi. She called me that night. I didn't say a word, but she knew I was listening. She told me she still missed me, she still loved me . . . and I didn't say a word." Unlike everyone else I've talked to, David spills this all without asking anything of me.

In his features, I see the collage on the wall of the storage room, the tunnel of photos in the lighthouse, the streams of memories she made in his name too. A million missed connections are hidden in melodies and memories.

I hold the key on my necklace close before I snap it off and extend it to him, sliding the inn's key off and giving him the other. "I think this was meant for you."

He wipes his eyes. "What is it?"

"A clue. She left a piece of her behind. She left the key at this house by the sea for you to find. There are two places you need to go, one this unlocks and one it doesn't. Trust me, they're worth seeking."

This nostalgic look takes over his features. "My family's old home. They moved. A few years ago."

Studying him for a second, I ask, "Can I show you something?" He didn't ask for anything, but I can give him something, show him how she's still here. I wave him forward.

He doesn't answer, but he follows—still wiping his tears.

"Where are we going?" he says about halfway to the stage, down the aisles.

"Stand on the stage," I say, and I begin to climb to the catwalk alone.

"Is this what you were doing in my theater the other day?" There's almost a joking edge to this.

"Partially." I reach that spotlight she left for me, and I flick it on and watch as Tori Rose's rose-colored, rose-patterned glow falls upon him, sets him aflame in its light—her light.

He gawks. "How did she . . ."

"No one knows," I study it again. "Can you tell me a story? How did you get here?"

He speaks to the empty audience even as he speaks to me. "I couldn't do it. She proposed a summer of dreams, our Summer of Dreams. It was a whole thing. It's hard to explain." If only he knew how much I knew. "We were going to spend half of it in Nashville and half in New York. She never left Nashville, and I never got to New York. She didn't want to finish it with me, and I didn't want to finish it without her. Like I said, we fell apart. When we parted, I came back here and moped around a while. I starred in community theater. That time I saw her . . . I regret nothing more than I regret not going to her. I don't know just how badly seeing her shook me, but that was my last show.

"After that, I went around the country to her concerts, and

I watched her be a star like I always said I would. I realized it quickly. I guess I knew the songs were about me and her and us, but I never got up the nerve to call back, and she never came to me again. Every once in a while, I'd convince myself she saw me in the crowd. When she returned, she reunited with Patrick. They kept their fling secret, but this town knew. Sunset Cove can hide anything from the world.

"I took over the theater after my favorite director passed, bless his soul. I ran some shows, and then I didn't. Now it's just upkeep."

His story joins with hers, with Patrick's, with Edie's, with Sara's, with my grandmas', with Linnea's, with mine. They all paint her in different ways, so no one person could complete her image alone.

"You should start again." I lean forward. "I'm sure there was something in my mom's letter about keeping your dreams."

He shields his eyes from the red spotlight, and he looks at me even though I'm sure he can't really make me out up here on the catwalk. His eyes tell me I'm right about what she said. "Maybe I will. You want to help?"

"I'm sorry. I can't. I have a dream of my own to chase." I have a girl I hope to chase it with, to follow into the sunset and sunrise and every summer after this one if she'll still have me, if my fear and denial weren't too much. "You got a play in mind?"

"Yeah," he says, gentle and fond. "*Summer of Dreams—The Story of Tori Rose*. It's time this town learns the whole story. Sees her and loves her for all of her, not just the fame."

My heart skips. "Can I read it?"

"Sure. I've got it somewhere. I wrote it years ago."

"I think she'd like that."

"You remind me of her, you know?" this boy—David Summers—from my mom's past says, still looking at me.

I smile softly. "So I've been told."

MIA

Grams says Mom liked roses best of all flowers—as unsurprising as that is—and we take them to her grave together at noon.

"I'm glad you finally got to know her," Grams says, a hand on my back. Her jewelry is scarlet today, and her dress matches. She told me Mom asked the whole town to dress in that color for her funeral and that Sunset Cove was draped in rose red for the whole week. "She was something special. She was a song of her own." She and Nana have been sprinkling tales of my mother's childhood into every minute they can like they want to get enough in to make up for lost time.

I love them for the days they speak of her, and even with the pain it drew between us, I love them for the days they don't, the days they can't too.

"She was so many songs," I agree.

Grams presses an affectionate kiss to my temple. "So many. I wish she could see us now. Me and Nana married. You all grown up."

"She sang about it. She imagined it. That counts for something."

"Look at you befriending silver linings."

I pat the guitar that rests against my chest—a pink that matches my top and the flowers stitched across the hips of my blue jeans. The instrument has become a part of me too. "I have big plans for tonight. I figure believing a little bit might give me some good luck."

"You don't need luck." I need so much of it, desperately. I guess she sees that in my expression because she links her hand through mine and pulls away. "I'll leave you to it."

"Thank you," I mouth as she walks away, and she flashes the sign for *I love you* over her shoulder, like we've done since I was little. I make the same gesture and watch her in her red clothes, walking through gravestones and brushing away tears.

She's out the gate of the Sunset Cove Cemetery before I even sit on the grass.

The roses faintly taint the air, and I breathe them in as I read her headstone.

TORI ROSE PETERS

1971–2006

MAY YOU REST IN MUSIC

It's like I'm eight years old again, finally brave enough to come here and look at this but not wise enough to comprehend her loss, just to know that I was missing something—missing a presence that could only be filled by her.

"Hi, Mom," I say like I did the day I opened her diary. "I miss you. Thank you for everything you did for me. You aren't even here, and you taught me about courage and dreams and going after what I want. You showed me it wasn't easy and that you regretted things, but that was part of it. I wish you could see me. I want to try every day to make you proud. I'll remember you. Forever.

"I've been thinking about everything you told me. About last love songs. I thought about how you gave yours to me. I don't know when my last love song will be. I hope I don't know for a long time, but I also know stuff is unpredictable, and maybe I'll be like you and I'll find out sooner than I want to. I can't stop that from happening any more than I can stop myself from feeling or stop the music inside me or stop missing you. I really do miss you.

"What I can stop, hopefully, is another heartbreak. I met this girl. I've known her since I was born, and I've been kissing her for what feels like forever, but I keep messing it up. I haven't been fair, and I hurt her, and I hope this song is a beginning not the end because I love her. I do. And I'm done hiding. I wanted to share it with you."

Sitting crisscross in the cemetery, I take a deep breath and strum the first few chords. I let the music flow, and I share with her what might be my last song for the girl of my dreams, but what might also be the start of a new journey between us.

I hope, with every bone in my body—in this skeleton I'm still piecing together of who I am—that it's the latter and that she'll give me one final chance.

MIA

In what may be hopelessly tragic Romeo and Juliet fashion—even more so than climbing the vine-patterned trellis outside Britt's house as I've done for years—I throw pebbles at her window under the glow of the blue motion detector. My guitar is still across my back after my song to the graveyard. My hopes are in my back pockets.

After the fourth pebble, the window slides open and she leans all the way out, already annoyed. "What do you want, Mia? I'm trying to sleep."

It's nine at night, and the last time she went to bed this early was after she pulled an all-nighter waiting for an album to drop.

"I need to talk to you. I'll go after this. You don't have to say anything. I just need to tell you how wrong I was. You were right."

"I always am." There's an assuredness in her eyes, and I think it's the reason I fell in love with her in the first place—why I still am and will always be. I don't want to be in my fifties and crying in a theater because I let love slip away. I want it now, and I want it with her, and I need to have not ruined the best thing to ever happen to me.

"I was scared," I say. "You're used to that, and I don't blame you for being sick of it because it's not fair to you. It's not fair to ask you to wait for me, to keep you waiting." She stays silent, head in her hand, and lips pursed as she watches me from the window. She hasn't told me to fuck off yet, so I take that as a good sign. "I wanted the music and you so badly, but I got scared and I panicked, and I worried we'd end up with more regrets than happy endings."

She meets this revelation with a continuation of her silence.

I keep going. I take this opening to prove to her that there will never be a day I don't miss her, don't love her, don't sing for her. "I was wrong about my mom too. Again, you were right. I finished the hunt. She told me to chase my dreams."

"Mia," Britt cuts in, and my heart leaps. "I'm happy you figured things out, but I don't want an apology because someone else told you to follow your dreams. If you're here to tell me something real, say it. If you're here to tell me what she told you, you should go. I want you to want it. I'm not taking excuses."

She wants me to want it—does that mean she still wants me?

And I said I was sure last time, but I need to give her more than words, more than claims. I need to give her something real too.

I start pulling things from my pockets, and instead of envelopes containing my family's past, they're the building blocks of my own story—of the story I hope for with her. I hold them up one at a time. "I want to show you I mean it. I'm here in whatever way I can be. This is a list of sixteen suites in Nashville that would be affordable. This is a list of places in the heart of Nashville that are hiring right now so we can pay rent. This one is a list of the places where celebrities and country stars found their big breaks. These are recording studios and record labels as big goals for the future to keep us driving for something."

I continue pulling papers from my jeans, coat, purse,

unraveling more and more threads of this promise and saying, "These are the songs I've written, most about you, most today, missing you. And . . ." I pull the last thing out. "I called in a favor. I reached out to the Bluebird Café as her daughter, and you have a gig there too. People go there for the music, people go there for discovery. It's under your name, not mine. It's for you and your songs, wherever we end up. I want you to have it. I want you to have your dream even if it doesn't include me. I want you to have everything." And I do. If she tells me after all this to leave, I will. I'll have to let her go.

She's watching me, studying me, staring at me, and not saying a word.

I say, "I have one last thing. A last *promise* to you to show you how sure I am about Music City, this dream, everything if you still want me. I learned recently that everyone gets a last love song, and, Britt Garcia, my last love song will always be to you."

With that, I sit down beneath the weeping willow, and I sing up to her window and hope the tune and the apologies reach her.

Most people don't find forever at eighteen,
'Till death do we part' too much a cage,
For loosely tied strings and young, wild hearts,
But for her I would toss 'for now' to the wind,
Forever becoming my epiphany, my long-lost dream,
The pillars of my heart built on the grounds of this
timeless word,
Anything to make it true.

Because I met a girl, in a nowhere town,
Where the ocean stretches far and dreams come to
drown,

I met a girl who taught me to rise when the sun goes down,
I met a girl who was every constellation in the endless sky,
I met a girl who resurrected my hopes when I'd sent them to die,
I met a girl who showed me the other side of the horizon,
I met a girl who taught me that maybe love could be relied on,
And I was young, I was broken, I was fragmented and scared,
But I met a girl and she taught me forever comes when you dare,
So, yes, my vows of forever come at only eighteen,
But for her I would promise any damn thing.

I would repaint the sky, make the stars spell her name,
Gamble with the moon to beg her to stay,
I would slay mysteries and dragons and the lies that tore us apart,
Just to never hurt her, never break her star-woven heart.
And in this forever at only eighteen,
I want to follow the music with her, want to follow this dream.

I collect my breath, and the last stars wink out with those notes, loveless as I made them, but when I look up, some of the coldness has faded from her eyes.

"What's it called?" she asks, completely unreadable.

"'Britt Garcia, I'm Sorry and You Will Always Be Right'?"

She almost laughs, almost smiles, but she's still watching, waiting. "No, really, what's it called?"

"Forever 18."

"I think we found the missing song of Lost Girls's set when we go to Nashville together. Don't you agree?"

My heart jumps over the music and into her hands. "Wait, are you serious? Britt, I don't have to be part of that. I know I didn't show up and Amy and Sophie probably hate me. I let you down. All of—"

"Oh, I have conditions." She leans forward through the window.

That sounds about right. "Whatever they are, you've got it." I set my mother's guitar—now mine—down between the weeds and wildflowers growing in her lawn.

"You might want to hear them first."

"I agree to them all. Anything for you. I meant what I said in the song."

She raises all five fingers, and I smile a little. "First, I get to be right for our next five fights. No questions asked."

"I'm in."

"Second, you get the afternoon shifts driving to Nashville because it's hot and I like to drive when the stars are out."

"No problem."

"Third, we are leaving tomorrow and you have to make a packing list and submit it to me tonight because you're forgetful and I'm not sharing my food or my toothbrush." Her smile is starting.

"All right." I laugh.

"Fourth, you sing that song whenever you apologize. It's the only apology I will accept from now on." The first real emotion shows, and we both choke up.

I take a step closer to the window, closer to her. She's the only person I am fully able to recklessly believe in because she's the only one who comes through time and time again. "I can do that."

"Fifth, you never back out on me, on us, on any band I get you into or song you promise me again. You need to be real sure this time. You will never make me walk away from you again. It was hard, Mia. Let's not lose each other."

"I never want to lose you. I'm sorry. I'm so sorry for everything."

"Lastly—"

I smile at her, and now she's smiling back and I can breathe. "I thought there were five conditions?"

"I made one more."

"And that is?"

She leans a little closer. "Lastly, you come up here and kiss me."

"I can do that," I say, and I climb the trellis to her one last time. I grin beneath the starlight, and I have never made so many discoveries and loved so many people in a way I know could break me, but I'm willing to risk it. It's terrifying, but I angle forward, and I kiss her in this night of promises.

She kisses me back, and we fall inside through her window.

"I love you," I whisper. "I love you." When I say it, it's all I feel, and I'm no longer running from it.

"I love you too," she says, and I kiss her harder, and she kisses me right back again.

As we become this eternity, this song, this melody, whatever burns between us is brighter than the fear, and the loveless stars that tore me apart no longer stand a chance.

EPILOGUE
MIA

Today, I bring the roses on my own, and I set them against my mother's tombstone, with the already wilting ones from the day before. With them, I leave a letter, and I step back to stand by Britt, lacing my fingers through hers and taking one last look at the sea beyond the gates of the cemetery, the true horizon of Sunset Cove, after which everyone's favorite diner coined its name.

"We're doing this," I say to Britt, to myself, to my mother, to this town.

Britt's the only one who responds, with a squeeze of my hand and a whisper that turns to a shout near the end. "We're finally getting out of here." She kisses my cheek, and I grin because the dream is in reach after all, and I'm reaching *for* it.

For someone who says so many goodbyes, though, the goodbyes this morning and this one now shouldn't be so hard. My grandmas and I had our longest-running movie night yet after I submitted my list and loaded my bags, and I was exhausted by the time I finished hugging them and dragged my suitcase down the hall. I walked out the front door to air that smelled like possibility in some weird way.

Linnea gave me and Britt free coffee for our journey and hugged us both so tight I almost didn't let her go. We had a last song at the karaoke machine—just Britt and I. Linnea made us promise to call, and then we left the Horizon for what might be the final time in who knows how long.

My father, Patrick Rose, called me this morning, whether that be coincidence or the fate my mother claimed had them meet in the first place. I said I might take him up on his offer to stop by his house on the coast one day, to say hi and maybe to yell at him in person before I let him hear a little bit of my story.

Edie was next, and I got to talk to her for a good fifteen minutes before Britt pulled me out the door and I kissed her outside Back to Me & You. We raced to her house where we had lunch with Amy, Sophie, and her parents before coming here to the cemetery for what might be my toughest goodbye of the day.

With the sea whistling behind me, I step forward, press my fingers to my lips. I touch them to her grave. "See you in the stars, Mom."

Britt's hand brushes my back and her eyes are gleaming. "Mia, we're really doing this."

"We're doing this," I echo her purposefully, and I'm every bit as sure. I wrap my arms around her to kiss her in this town one last time before the open road.

"Let's go," she says, nodding toward where the rest of Lost Girls waits at the gate—*our* band. It's going to take some time proving I'll show up, making it up to them before they fully forgive me, but I plan to keep earning my place every day.

I nod and glance at the note under the bundle of fresh flowers. Then I grab Britt's hand, and she pulls me near, and together we race off into the last sunset of this summer and beyond.

Behind me, I leave the words—my story—for my mother in thanks for everything.

It all began the summer I was Mia Peters and I found the diary you left me. It began when I had unanswered questions and a heart scared to love and all the wrong melodies beating inside of me. It began the summer I first went with the music and the girl of my dreams, and I learned I wasn't leaving them any time soon.

It all began when I followed your story to find my own.

ACKNOWLEDGMENTS

Thank you so much for reading *The Last Love Song* and spending time with Mia and the rest of Sunset Cove. This book is so much of my hope, fear, and love, and it exists because of some truly incredible people who I'm so excited to get this chance to thank.

To Alex Rice who is the fiercest advocate, the kindest human, and one of my favorite people. I'm incredibly grateful that the *yes* that made my dreams come true came from you. Thank you as well to Bianca Petcu, Marine Adzhemyan, Kathryn Driscoll, and everyone at Creative Artists Agency who makes the agency feel like home.

Daniel Ehrenhaft, I couldn't stop grinning the first time you signed off an email with "your fan," and it has remained an absolute joy and honor to have you as an editor; I am such a fan of you! Thank you, Ember Hood for the amazing copy edits, and Katrina Tan and Adrienne Roche for all your work on this book. To Tatiana Radujkovic and Francie Crawford for your insight, support, and excitement. To Larissa Ezell for the capturing my book so perfectly in the most beautiful cover and making it so pretty inside and out. To Josh Stanton and Brendan Deneen, *thank you* doesn't feel like enough for all of your support for this book. I am truly so lucky to be published by Blackstone.

Thank you to the writing community for the wonderful enthusiasm this story has received from the start. I am so appreciative of everyone who read early pages and drafts, boosted my pitches, or left encouraging comments. To Rosiee Thor and K. Kazul Wolf for helping me hone my craft and to Rosiee again for all your lovely guidance even years later. To Jordan Kelly for teaching me so much about writing and publishing. To Camille Simkin who was the first person to read this book and who gave the most amazing edit letter. To Emma Baker for your kindness and brilliant notes. To Emily Charlotte, *The Last Love Song* may actually just be a scavenger hunt for cameos of you. To Leah Jordain, one of the best authors and people I know; your insightful edits make me a better writer every single time, and your friendship means the world. To Shana Targosz, who always makes me smile. To Janice Davis, who once called herself the Miss Honey (feat. knives and Shibas) to my Matilda; I freaking adore you. To Zoulfa Katouh, who has the most beautiful heart and books. To Jenna Miller for your friendship and support. To Jenna Voris for being my April sapphic-country-music-book twin. To Safa Ahmed, Ann Zhao, Sydney Langford, Arushi Avachat, Trinity Nguyen, Alina Khawaja, and Christy Healy, who I'm so excited to debut alongside and who helped me get to 2024. To De Elizabeth who is one of the reasons I survived the sub trenches / great war. To Aymen Ali, whose art blows me away and who created the most incredible postcard for this book. To Arin for the amazing preorder print. To Tiffany Wang for the PowerPoint that is one of the kindest things anyone has ever made me. To Author Mentor Match Round 6 for being my first writing community and making me feel the most welcome. To Alex Felix, Gabrielle Bonifacio, Aarti Gupta, Aza, Brighton Rose, M. K. Lobb, Natalie Sue, Lindsey Hewett, Savannah Wright, Cristin Williams, Nicole Chartrand, Christie Megill, Page Powars, Ellie Blackwood, Marcella, Hannah Bahn, Cath Tseng, Layla Noor, Laila Sabreen, Sophie Wan, Chelsea Abdullah, Britney Shae Brouwer, Eric Smith, Elle Gonzalez Rose, Lauren Kay, Tamar Voskuni, Taleen Voskuni, Victoria Wlosok, Brian D. Kennedy, Riss M. Neilson, Anna Gracia, Susan Azim Boyer, M. K. Pagano, Ambika Vohra, Bethany Baptiste, and Hadley Leggett for all of your support. To three incredible authors who consistently remind me why I love books so much and who let me be part of theirs: Safa Ahmed (again), Evelyn Ding, and Kaitlin Stevens. To the beans group chat: Nadia Noor, Sophia Hannan, Theresa Fettes, Rania Singla, and Birdie Schae. I love you all so much. To Addie Yoder for bringing so much light and joy to my entire family's lives. And to Tara Creel who is family at this point and has read my first book, this one, and all the ones in between.

Thank you to so many authors I look up to who have looked out for me. To Courtney Kae for your kindness, advice, and so much more. Thank you for being my conference buddy and incredible friend and literally the most wonderful human. To Carolina Flórez-Cerchiaro and Jennie Wexler for believing in me and this book from so early on. To Christina Li for answering an anxious sixteen-year-old's fangirling DM. To Catherine Bakewell for being so wonderful and giving the best pep talks. To Emily Wibberley and Austin Siegemund-Broka for being my first blurb, amazing friends, and two of the coolest people I've ever met. To Jessica Parra for literally everything; I adore you. To Kyla Zhao, who surprised me with pastries when I announced this book deal and has been the absolute loveliest to me always. To Jacqueline Firkins, who is so amazingly talented. To Jennifer Probst, who invited me to hang out with the authors in the lobby. To Dahlia Adler, Nina Moreno, Rachael Lippincott, and Bridget Morrissey for taking the time to read *The Last Love Song* and say such lovely things.

Thank you to the friends who make me feel worthwhile on my worst days and my best. To Ananya Devarajan for more than I can put into words; thank you for believing in me from the start, for your immeasurable kindness, and for the love and care you put into every moment of our friendship. To Birdie Schae for being my ride-or-die. I love our chaotic phone calls and screaming texts and can't wait to meet you IRL one day. To Caitlin Cross who I don't think I've been able to go a day without texting in four years. There's no one I'd rather have as a mentorship-turned-self-adopted sister and querying and sub bestie; I will never stop feeling lucky that you've stuck with me all this time. To Gwen Lagioia who is the best writing partner and friend; all of my favorite drafting memories are of us trying to align our lives and time zones to sneak in sprints together. To Leila Dizon because David and I love you and you've probably read this story more times than anyone else. To Swati Hegde for the late-night talks, unwavering friendship, and looking out for me like both a sister and a best friend; I am so grateful to know you. I love you all so much.

To the people in my offline life who remind me to be present. To Ana Mara for the kind of genuine, fulfilling, hilarious, and life-affirming friendship I can hardly begin to describe. To the Mara family for the care and thoughtfulness with which you approach life. To Brittany Machado, who's an author bestie I've been lucky enough to hang out with online and offline. To Colby for supporting my writing for so long. To Robyn, Maddy, and Piper for making me feel at home at university for the first time.

To Rya, Faith, and Emily for being so supportive of this book. To Emili for in-person writing sprints and talks. To Sydney for turning lyrics from this book into the most beautiful music. To Eva for always being there for me and being such an amazing friend. To Nishayla for our car-ride chats, *Twilight* movie nights, and years of friendship.

To the teachers who nurtured my love of writing and saw something in me when I was still learning to see something in myself. To Tammie Chernoff for the days you let me stay late in your classroom when I was anxious, your mentorship, and your belief in me; thank you for always leading with your entire heart. To Nicole Dyck who is a brilliant, kind and empathetic person and educator; I am so grateful for all the times you went above and beyond to support me. To Catherine Davies, Eilidh MacConnell, and Brenda Hatson for making the library feel like home. To Shane Mummery and Matt Greenfield for making the subject I've always stressed the most about something I looked forward to. To Krystie Shirlaw who always believed in me and my books; thank you for giving me a place to sit and write them. To Trisha Lumsden and Kayt Etsell for being my safe spaces at school; your impact extends far beyond the classroom. To Michelle Superle and Brett Pardy for being such amazing profs and my go-to for as many courses as I can take.

To the musicians whose songs have inspired me for so long. Thank you, especially to Kelsea Ballerini and Taylor Swift, whose music has always been there for me.

To my family; I love you beyond words. To Grammy for being my first best friend and spending so many hours with me, especially those ones winding up music boxes so I could hear their tunes. To Nana, who's one of the strongest people I know, for the lunches and introducing me to *Mamma Mia!*. To Auntie Brenda for being the coolest aunt and best person to swap book recommendations with. To Uncle Dave, Jack, and Violet for being three of my favorite people in the world. To Grampy and Papa for believing in me. To Denise and Ira for laughter, love, and songs around the guitar. To Brent, Brandon, and Amy, for making me family to begin with.

To Riley for an unquantifiable number of things that are part of the also-unquantifiable number of reasons I love you. For the movie nights and late-night talks. For being my safe place and person. For helping me believe I deserve good things and making me believe in love stories again. For your excitement and kindness and passions and interests and insights and support and your love that I somehow got lucky enough to be on the receiving end of every day. I love you. You know.

And to the people who made me who I am today. To Dad for being my coach, the funniest person I've ever met, the rock of our family, the person who pushes me to be the best I can be and showed me growing up what love should look like. If Mia had a dad half as amazing as you are, there probably wouldn't be a book here. To Ames for being my built-in bestie since you were born; you make me a better friend, person, and sister by existing and light up every space you're in; being your big sister is one of the best things I've ever gotten to be. And to Mum, who is my hero. I've never been able to sum up how much you mean to me in a birthday card or Mother's Day message, so here, I wrote a whole book to try; this one's always been for you.

MY PLAYLIST

Writing *The Last Love Song* tapped into so many little corners of my heart, and one of my favorite parts of the process was working on the original lyrics, woven throughout. The book is structured around its own playlist—a discography that exists inside the story. Outside of this story world, every time I would try to fall back into Mia and Tori's lives after being away from the keyboard, I had a playlist of songs I love to kept me company, and I'm excited to get to share these with you.

You'll find a mix of genres, decades, and artists—and of course a track from *Mamma Mia! Here We Go Again*—but I think Kelsea Ballerini, Taylor Swift, and Maisie Peters take the reign. Unsurprisingly, they're also in the top five of my Spotify Wrapped each year. These artists in particular have provided me solace and such a safe space for so long. When I was fifteen going through my first heartbreak, I had Kelsea Ballerini on repeat. When I was falling in love for the first time, it was along to a series of Taylor Swift love songs. And Maisie Peters is always there for the unique existential crisis of fumbling through your early twenties.

In *The Last Love Song*, Mia connects with Tori through the songs she's written. I find pieces of myself in music as much as in books. And I hope you'll find something in this story and this accompanying playlist that'll keep playing in your heart after you turn the last page.

—Kalie Holford

SCAN THE QR CODE TO LISTEN

TO THE PLAYLIST THAT INSPIRED THE NOVEL